I0460814

Between the Lanterns

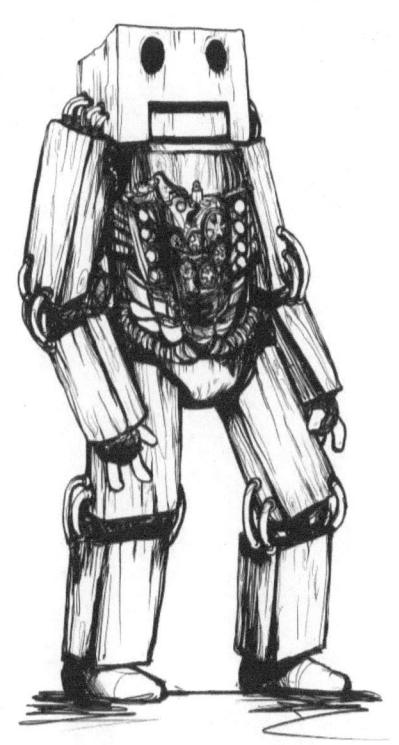

J.M. BUSH

MilkMan Publishing

Copyright © 2016 James Michael Bush, MilkMan Publishing
All rights reserved. This Book or any portion thereof may not be reproduced or used in any manner whatsoever without the express written permission of the publisher, except for the use of brief quotations in a book review. This is a work of fiction. Names, characters, businesses, places, events and incidents are either the products of the author's imagination or used in a fictitious manner. Any resemblance to actual persons, living or dead, or actual events is purely coincidental.

Edited by Matt Rance @ Proof Professor
Cover design by Stefanie Saw @ Seventh Star
Interior artwork created by Ammar Khalifa

Printed in the United States of America

First Printing, 2016

ISBN: 0-9972842-2-6
ISBN-13: 978-0-9972842-2-5

MilkMan Publishing
914 El Dorado Drive
Dothan, AL 36303

www.eatplaywritetravel.com

This book is dedicated to my hometown, Dothan, Alabama. I resented you when I was young, but now I understand what makes you great. Distance makes the heart grow fonder, as they used to say, and I've been about as far away from you as possible for a long time.

ACKNOWLEDGMENTS

I'd like to thank everyone who bought my last novel. The outpouring of positivity from readers has been incredible. I hope that this book can match and surpass the success of Storm in Shanghai. In addition, I would like to thank my beta readers for Between the Lanterns: Brad Clayton, Candace Strickland, and my wife Merissa Lulling Bush. With the feedback I received from you, this novel went from pretty good to wonderful, and I am forever in your debt for that.

Perhaps most importantly for this particular novel, I would like to thank my friend Bobby Lee Hill, whose song "In Between the Lantern" inspired the story found within these pages. Your music has always made my heart dance, and I hope that I did your beautiful lyrics justice with this book.

Between the Lanterns

PREFACE

They met between the lanterns on West Main Street. The ones at the very end of the downtown strip of shops, all the way down past the bars and restaurants. All the way down past the clinic, the Baptist church, and the new office buildings. Those two lanterns hung in the air, levitating like all the other ones in New Dothan. There was nothing special about them. They gave off the same light as the others fueled by the Tesla generator outside of town, providing pure, clean, wireless energy. No poles were holding them in place. The magnetic levitation plates on the bottom kept them at the perfect ten feet above the automated sidewalks. They were normal, everyday lanterns. And that is where they met for the very first time.

Samantha was returning home from a long day waiting tables at Cheryl's Diner. A throwback to the old days, reminiscent of the food you would find at Waffle House…when those still existed. The food was probably the best in town. Home-style cooking made with love, heart, and soul. Most of the people in New Dothan wouldn't eat there, though.

1

Cheryl's Diner still used real meat, real vegetables, and real, home-made bread — all of the ingredients obtained from a small farm in Headland Town, where the last remaining farmers in the area still held onto the old ways.

Nowadays most everyone had a Nutricator in their homes. A technological marvel, as they advertised Nutricator, could create whatever you wanted to eat using processed protein and fiber to provide a nutritious meal for the whole family. Ask for pizza, you get it. Hamburgers? Sure. Duck à l'orange even. The problem was, it was all fake.

Samantha hated food from a Nutricator. She loved taking the time to break ingredients down and then use them to create something that took time and patience. She felt that Nutricator food was bland. It only "kinda sorta reminded you of what you really wanted," she was fond of saying. But it was quick, easy, and most importantly, it was popular.

August was on his way to the hardware store. He had just rented a new apartment out past the end of West Main Street and was trying to fix the place up. It was a dump, sure, but it was his dump. It was all he could afford from his meager wages working on the line of the industrial factory outside of town. The one where they made all the major components for everything computerized in the area. They built the chips, motherboards, controllers, and activators for just about every modern device available. They were part of a world-wide conglomerate that owned almost everything and everyone. Montek paid their employees extremely low wages, even though they were a financial giant, which is why August could barely afford his tiny, run-down apartment.

As they walked down the street, both avoided the automated sidewalks because, well... legs were made for walking... not standing idle. So they strode towards one another from opposite ends of West Main. The moment they crossed between the lanterns, all of the lights in town went out.

Samantha and August each gasped loudly at the exact moment utter darkness fell upon New Dothan. Instinctively, they both reached out for something... anything to hold onto. Their hands connected in the dark and their fingers intertwined like the wool woven into an intricately patterned sweater.

"Don't worry, I've got you. I'm here," August blurted out for some reason.

"And who might you be, sweets?" Samantha said, adding, "And may I ask why you are holding my hand?"

She grinned saying this, feeling no threat coming from the man in the dark. Samantha had seen him coming towards her, and he was a rather attractive fellow. Probably in his mid-twenties, with very dark skin like that of a West African, close-cut hair, and an average physique; neither fat, trim, nor athletic - just somewhere deliciously in the middle. His eyes were bright, and his face was gorgeous.

August had no idea that it was a woman in the dark until she had spoken to him. He felt rather embarrassed now at having said what he did, not to mention he was still holding her hand... But then again, she was still holding his hand right back. He now wished that he had been paying attention, so he would know what she looked like.

But August, as usual, had been lost in his thoughts. Often he thought of song lyrics, or sometimes stories, but mostly he just imagined himself anywhere but living in New Dothan. It's not that he hated the town. In fact, he thought it was full of decent enough people, even if they flocked to buy any new gadget on the market while throwing out tried and true traditions like yesterday's potato chips. The history of New Dothan was also rich with great characters and steeped in wonderful stories of kindness; even if most of the residents had forgotten them all.

No, it wasn't the specific town of New Dothan that bothered him. It was just that he had always lived there. August had never, not even once, left the Wiregrass area. So it was pretty much all he wanted out of life these days — to save enough Credit and find a way to travel the world.

Just as August was wishing that he knew what this mystery woman looked like, the lights in New Dothan came back on as suddenly as they were extinguished a minute before. And August almost fell down from the shock of seeing her.

It felt like getting hit by a truck. It felt like for his entire life up until that point there had been a giant hole in August's chest, but with just one look at the shining light of this woman's face that abyss became full, even if only temporarily.

This feeling wasn't mere sexual attraction, either. He felt no animalistic urges to lie down with this gorgeous lady and continue the overpopulation of planet Earth. It was something much deeper than that, and more painful, too. It was agony and nirvana at the same time. She looked at August, and he felt that nothing, no matter what else he ever accomplished in his pathetic life, would ever be as wonderful as when she looked at him.

"Are you ok, sweets?" Samantha asked.

August could only stare for a moment, before stuttering in reply, "Uh, what? Sorry... what'd you say?"

Samantha smiled. It felt good to be noticed by an attractive man.

"I said, are you ok?" she repeated herself. "You're staring, you know?"

August realized he was making a fool of himself in front of the most beautiful woman he had ever seen. She wasn't beautiful by the standards of modern insane media. She was nothing like all the women he saw in movies and on TV, who were too thin and plastic. And, just like food from a Nutricator, they were all fake. These women may have been composed of organic parts, but a machine had artificially assembled those parts; they weren't natural.

This woman, though, with her straight, shoulder-length black hair, almond-shaped eyes, that perfect skin tone that only East Asians could obtain, and the small spread of freckles across her face: she was radiant like a sun.

Not Earth's sun, though. It was too dim to describe her. No, she was radiant like the sun of a distant planet that could melt the Earth from across the galaxy. Of course, the way that navy blue dress with white dots all over it fit the delicate curves of her small breasts and backside was also quite compelling to the young man.

"Hello?" Samantha said. "You're still staring. Kinda freaking me out there, sweets. Are you ok, for real? Did the blackout fry your brains or something?"

"Am I ok?" August dumbly asked, "I ain't sure, to be honest. But I think now that I've seen you, I could be. I'm…" He cut off abruptly.

August almost gave her his name. Almost. But he had been rejected and broken his whole life. Not just by women, but also by co-workers, his parents, and his friends; even his dog had run away. So, he decided not to open himself up for more heartbreak.

"I… I'm fine, ma'am," he stuttered. "I'm sorry for spacin' out like that. I'll take off now. That is if you're ok?"

Samantha smiled even wider. She thought this boy was too damn cute. "Yes, sweets. I'm alright," she said kindly. "Thanks for your concern."

"Ok, great. Great. Well, I'll, uh, stop wastin' your time, then," August told her.

"See you around." August realized he sounded foolish, but he couldn't help it.

She was that entrancing.

"I hope so, sweets. Maybe we'll meet between the lanterns again," Samantha said, and she meant it. He was put together real well and seemed like a very nice man.

August, too, sincerely hoped they would meet again.

CHAPTER 1
THAT AIN'T FOOD

Several weeks passed. Samantha continued to work away at the diner. It had been six years since she had started working there. It wasn't glamorous, and it barely paid the bills. But none of that mattered to Samantha. She was happy making real food. She was pleased to make anything with her hands, actually.

When she was off work, she made origami swans or paintings of the night sky. Sometimes she attempted woodworking. Sam found that very satisfying and she was getting pretty good at it. The sense of satisfaction in taking some wood and turning it into whatever she could imagine was wonderful.

Sometimes she made figurines of fish or bears. Other times she tried bigger projects, like the bookcase in her living room. Maybe it was a little bit crooked, but she hadn't gone down to Montek.Mart and bought it. Samantha had made it with her own two hands, and that was worth a few books falling down every once in a while.

One afternoon at work, the diner was unusually busy. Most of the time they only had ten to fifteen customers all day, but on this day all twenty seats in the restaurant were full, and two more people were waiting outside for a table to open up.

"Tara, why on Earth is it so busy today?" Samantha asked with wide eyes.

"I have no clue, Sam! Isn't it wonderful?" her co-worker and financial partner, Tara, replied. "I wish every day could be like this. With tips like this, I could afford a Nutricator for my apartment within a week!"

"Why in Heaven's name would you want a stupid old Nutricator, Tara?" Samantha asked, truly disgusted. "That ain't food. That is just glued-together by-products. It's sick is what it is, sweets."

"Oh hush, Sam," Tara replied. "Not everyone loves to spend hours making dinner every night. Hell, I work in a diner: the last thing I want to do when I get home is cook more damn food. Anyway, take this pie over to table 10, please and thank you."

She could not understand why a woman like Tara, who could cook every bit as well as Samantha, would buy a damn Nutricator. It made no sense at all. But different strokes for different folks, they used to say. She grabbed the chocolate pie and headed over to table 10, where sat a lonely old man sipping a cup of freshly brewed Folgers.

"Here you are, sweets: a delicious slice of chocolate pie," Samantha said, laying the plate on the table. "I'm so jealous of you! Now I might have to eat a slice on my break in just a bit. You enjoy it, now."

The elderly man smiled at her with tears in his eyes and looked down in shame. Samantha couldn't begin to wonder why this gentle, older man would be so sad.

"I'm sorry, ma'am," he said through the frog in his throat. "I just realized that I only have enough Credit for the coffee. It sure does look delicious, though. My apologies, Miss."

He started to get up and gather his coat to leave, but Samantha was not about to allow this old gentleman to leave the diner on an empty stomach. She couldn't really afford to buy him the slice, and there was no way Tara would let her give it away. Samantha was just going to have to hope she wouldn't get caught.

"You sit right on down and eat this pie, sweets," she whispered in his ear. "It's on the house since you're such a handsome fellow. Just don't tell the boss lady, ok?"

Tara wasn't technically the boss; she was just in charge of the financial side of the diner. But he didn't need to know all that, so Samantha winked at the old man and he grinned bigger than he had for years.

Even if she did get caught, even if she had to pay for the slice of Cheryl's Famous Chocolate Pie out of her tips for today... she felt it was damn sure worth it just for that warm smile.

"Thank you so much, ma'am. I really do appreciate your kindness," the old man said. "I wish there were more good people like you in this world."

Samantha rubbed his shoulder and leaned down to whisper again in his ear, "Just between you and me, sweets? I don't plan on paying for this pie. So, actually, could stealing a piece of pie for a stranger be considered kind? I'm not so sure."

"Honestly, ma'am, right now I can't think of any kinder act in the entire world. Thank you, again," he said softly, not wanting to get the nice waitress in trouble.

She gave his old shoulder a pat, tossed him one last wink, and headed off to fill more cups and take away some plates.

-

August was on his way back to the hardware store. Again. In the past few weeks since they had first met, he had really gotten his apartment in decent shape. August had fixed all of the light fixtures, so they all had access to the wireless Tesla generator, instead of just the one in the kitchen and bedroom. That was a welcome fix, as now he could use the bathroom at night without... unfortunate consequences.

He had patched the holes in the walls and put down some throw rugs to cover the scratches on the floor. Most bachelors would either be wealthy enough to stay at a much nicer place, or just not care one bit about a crummy-looking apartment. August just liked to do something with his time, honestly. He loved to work with his hands. He wasn't much of a maker yet. August wanted to invent tech; he just didn't trust himself enough. He was pretty damn adept at fixing things, though. If something broke, August could make it work as good as new, or good enough.

He was pretty good at odd jobs and fixing up stuff at home, but August's real talent was with machines. That was funny to most people he knew because he didn't seem to like machines all that much. He didn't own a Nutricator for one. He also had a cellphone instead of a SmartChip. August refused to have one of those things implanted in his ear. He helped make them in the plant outside of town, and he saw how dirty some of the fingers were that touched those chips. "NO THANK YOU, SIR," he would say.

August had modified his cellphone to function like a SmartChip, though. It used Tesla power; so it never needed charging, and he connected it with the Montek.Communication satellite for free unlimited calls and Net surfing. It wasn't exactly legal, but no one would care if one little guy was piggybacking off of a multitrillion-dollar conglomerate.

Today he was headed back to the hardware store, not to buy anything, but to go out back and see if they had thrown anything useful away. It wasn't against the law to dumpster dive, and he had found a lot of great stuff back there before; like wood to fix his floor with, a handsaw to cut the wood, and lots of broken power tools that he could fix or take apart to scavenge pieces. He had no real plan or idea of what he wanted to find today; August was just bored and wanted something to do. He walked down West Main Street, just like he had every single day since the night he met her.

Every day he walked between the lanterns and looked for the beautiful Asian woman with freckled skin and shoulder-length hair that swished when she moved. He thought of her often. Her dark eyes with a bit of brown, her smile that was a little bit higher on one side, and the way she had called him "sweets." It was driving August crazy. He dreamed about this woman nightly, he thought about her while working on the assembly line at the plant, he pictured her sitting next to him while he ate his simple daily lunch of processed Nutricator sandwiches, provided free of charge by the company.

He had to find this woman. But August didn't know how. So for now, he walked down West Main Street every day hoping to see her again. As he walked down the road, avoiding the automated sidewalks, of course, his cellphone buzzed in his pocket. It was an automated message from Shop.Montek.Com.

Don't forget that today is the First Annual National Nutricator Day! We ask that you celebrate by supporting a local restaurant instead of using your Nutricator. While we appreciate your continued patronage of our wonderful products, we also want to help support local businesses like restaurants and hard-working farmers. To show our support, we've attached random amounts of Credit to each message sent out! Some will have enough to feed a family of ten and some only sufficient for a cup of coffee or a slice of pie! The only way to find out is to head to a local eatery, and check in! When you do, you'll receive Credit into your account earmarked only to be used at the restaurant where you checked in! Hurry up, though, as this offer is only good for today! HAPPY NATIONAL NUTRICATOR DAY!!!!

August shrugged his shoulders and decided that, although this was just some stupid marketing holiday, free food was free food. And this was REAL food. He opened an app called RFF, Real Food Finder, and searched for the closest non-Nutricator restaurant. The results showed a diner, a pub, and a Chinese restaurant.

The first was Cheryl's Diner, described as home-style cooking like your great-great-grandmother used to make. The second was Big Guy's Pub, touting the best real burgers and beers in town. A beer did sound nice right now. The third was Xiao Li's Kitchen and, apparently, was the only place in Alabama to get authentic Shanghainese food.

Well, Chinese food never sat very well with August for some reason. Probably because his diet consisted mostly of fake, cheap, Nutricator-made garbage, and Chinese food is so full of spices and sauces that it just upset the peaceful balance in his gut.

So it was really down to the pub or the diner. The pub had beer, which was a real draw for August. He hadn't had a real beer since his 21st birthday three years ago. The Nutricator beer served in most bars tasted like cardboard and only had an alcohol percentage of 2.1. It wasn't even worth the Credit, honestly. So a real beer sounded just plain amazing. The diner, though, well… it had chocolate pie.

CHAPTER 2
CHOCOLATE PIE

Chocolate pie. Just like his granny used to make for August when he was young. His parents may have been too hard on him and never supported any of his dreams or hobbies, but his granny had always nurtured in August the desire to work with his hands. She used to break her remote control for the TV so that August could fix it.

While he worked, she would make meat loaf, green beans, and biscuits for lunch. Afterward, she always had a slice of chocolate pie for him. August missed his granny a lot. She had died ten years before very suddenly when she had come down with the new cancer.

About thirty years ago, Montek.Pharm had cured all cancer. A single pill of their cure could eradicate cancer of any kind from anyone on Earth. And they had given the cure out for free. Montek didn't need the Credit, and so they used this as a marketing ploy. Give away the cure for cancer, and people will be loyal to you forever. It worked.

Years later, though, a new cancer started showing up in people of all ages, races, and tax brackets. No one could figure out where it came from or how to cure it. Montek's cure didn't even work. They tried over and over again to find a way to stop this cancer, but they just couldn't.

The good news was that it only affected about one in every 10,000 people at first. It was also not a painful way to die, as were the cancers of the past. It was the strangest disease ever to affect the human race. Basically, it was a timer set for death. Once diagnosed, the doctors could track it via the proteins in your blood the cancer attacked. You felt no pain at all. You could go on living your life just like normal, except for becoming a little bit forgetful. But once you contracted this cancer, you had an expiration date, and they could tell you the exact day you would die. For that reason, the disease came to be known as The Countdown.

When August's granny became sick, the doctor did all the tests and told her it was the new cancer. Once her Countdown had begun, the doc said it would be 27 days before her death. Exactly 27 days.

She never told August about it. He came and visited her several times over those last 27 days. He was older now, so she didn't break her remote control anymore. He would just come over and sit with Granny. They would talk for hours about her life, his dreams, or what he was building and fixing up. Granny would always tell him how proud she was of him.

His parents never once said to August that they were proud of him for anything. Granny told him every time they were together.

On day 27 she fixed him meat loaf, green beans, home-made biscuits, and of course… chocolate pie. After lunch, she hugged August tight and held it for an unusually long time.

"Granny, are you ok?" he asked. "What's the matter?"

"Not a thing, youngin. Not a thing," she lied to her grand-son. "I just love you ever so much. Have I told you how proud I am of the man you've become?"

"Yes, ma'am. You tell me all the time," he said. "Though I'm not sure what you're proud of me for doin'. I ain't never done anythin'. I ain't never even kissed a girl, Granny. I'm just a dud."

"Don't you dare ever say that about yourself again, you hear?" Granny scolded him. "You're a good man. You have a warm heart, a carin' soul, and you can do things with your mind and hands that most people couldn't ever dream of. You got more talent in your pinky than the entire Wiregrass area combined," she told him point-blank, and with a wag-ging finger for emphasis.

She went on to say, "One day you'll meet the right girl and y'all will be happier than anyone else ever has been. Listen to your granny, now. She knows everythin'."

"Yes, ma'am," August said respectfully. "Can I do anythin' around here before I head back home? Anythin' need fixin'?"

Granny smiled at August and started to cry. He had never once seen this strong, old woman cry. She wasn't unemotional; she was just tough as nails and only cried behind closed doors.

"Granny, really now," August said, worried to death, "what's the matter? Tell me. Whatever it is, I'll take care of it."

"Would that you could, August dear," Granny said sadly. "Would that you could. Now gimme a kiss, tell me you love me, and go live your life. You can't waste it all here with an old woman."

"Granny, I do love you," August said, planting a kiss on her wrinkled forehead. "Thanks for lunch. It was amazin' as usual. And, by the way, I'd be happy to stay here with you forever, rather than head back out there with all those rude, heartless sheep."

August leaned down and kissed his granny again, then walked out the door. The next time he saw her it was at her funeral two days later. He still felt heartbroken when he thought about it. Why hadn't she just told him?

Looking down at his cellphone displaying the description of the diner, and seeing Cheryl's Famous Chocolate Pie on the menu, August's eyes welled with tears. He closed the app and headed down the road to Cheryl's Diner.As he entered the little restaurant, he noticed there was seating for only around twenty people or so, and all the tables were full. Except for one. At one table sat an elderly man sipping on a cup of coffee and eating chocolate pie. It was a sign from his granny: he was sure of it.

"Excuse me, sir, would you mind very much if I sat with you and ate?" August asked the kindly-looking older man. "All the other tables are full up, and I'm gettin' pretty hungry."

The old gentleman looked up, still smiling from the kindness of the lovely young lady who had given him the pie, and said, "Well, one kind turn deserves another, as they used to say. Yes, sir, young man. Have a seat right there. And you have to try this pie, it is divine."

August grinned from ear to ear, stuck out his hand, and said, "Sir, I fully intend on it, I can promise you that. My name is August. How do you do?"

"Nice to meet you, August. My name is John, and I'm on cloud nine right now with this excellent coffee and delicious pie," the old fellow replied.

August thought that this old guy was just about the nicest person he had met in quite a while. To be honest, most people nowadays would have told August to get lost. The South used to be famous for good manners and warm welcomes, and people still acted a little bit kindly, but not as much as when August was a boy. And according to the stories Granny had told him, the people in today's world were right down cold and mean compared to the old days in Alabama.

As he looked at the menu, August's day got even better. The smile that spread across his face was infectious, and John couldn't help but make his smile bigger just to match.

"What's got you grinnin' like that, August?" John said warmly. "Find something other than pie on that there menu that sounds good?"

"Oh, John, I hope you don't think less of me if I cry while I eat. I'm about to order some meat loaf, green beans, homemade biscuits, and follow it all up with some chocolate pie. Just like my granny used to make me," August explained.

John put his fork down and wiped his mouth with a napkin. No longer smiling, but instead looking at August with affection in his wise, old eyes, he said, "August, that's probably the most incredible thing I've heard in years. If you cry when you eat, boy, I'm joinin' you. I came in here today because my ex-wife used to own this place. We divorced long before she started it, but when we were together, her cookin' was the best in town. When we separated, I moved down to Columbus, Georgia to work at Montek.Drive to build those AutoCars. I only just found out two days ago that she passed away from The Countdown a few years back. I never even knew, August. So, even though I got no Credit, I wanted to come down and see this place. I always meant to come down here and make good with her, you know? Well, the good Lord had other plans, I guess."

"John, I'm so sorry," August said with kindness. "My granny also passed from The Countdown. It's a damn shame. Pardon my language."

"Hell no, August. You're right. It is a damn shame. Anyway, I didn't have any Credit to eat here until I got that message from Montek about this National Nutri-whatever Day. I only wanted some coffee and some of Cheryl's chocolate pie. It was always my favorite. Only, once I checked in with my SmartChip, I found out that I only got enough for a cup of coffee. The pretty lady who works here gave me the pie for free out of the kindness in her heart like I ain't seen in years."

"Well, John, that was real sweet of her," August told his new friend. "I'll tell you what; let me check in and see how much they gave me and if it's enough, we can eat our fill of whatever we want. How's that sound to you?"

John smiled even bigger than before, if that was possible.

This was turning out to be the best day he had seen since before Cheryl left him.

"You know, August, I'd be ever so grateful for that," John said. "What say we take a look at your Montek Gift Credit?"

August grinned right back at John and opened his cellphone to check in. Almost immediately after checking in, he got a message from Montek.Credit and opened it. It was only enough for one cup of coffee.

"We're in luck, John," August lied, closing his phone quickly. "I hit the motherload. Order whatever you want, sir. It's on Montek today."

August could not really afford this, but there was no way he was going to let this kind old man down. He had enough saved up to buy himself a new workbench, but August would rather continue using his old, rickety workbench that he had fixed up on his own than deny John a big, wonderful meal.

CHAPTER 3
SPARKS FLY

Samantha came out of the kitchen with both arms full of plates. Earlier she had overheard one of the customers talking about National Nutricator Day, and the Credit that Montek was giving away for real food. Well, she might hate them and their stupid machines, but at least they were doing a good thing today. Even if it was just to lure more dummies into buying their useless garbage.

She handed out all the plates and chatted with a few customers. Most of them were not very talkative – nothing new there. People weren't friendly like they used to be, or so she had heard from Cheryl when Samantha started at the diner. That wonderful woman had always told of how things were in the old days in New Dothan.Cheryl had once said that running a diner was the best decision she ever made. Talking with the customers all day every day, making them smile with her meat loaf and chocolate pie, and being her own boss made Cheryl as happy as she had ever been. She told Samantha that her only regret was leaving her husband. Sure, he wasn't the most thoughtful man in the world, and he had messed up pretty bad, but Cheryl had loved him still, all the way until the end. She had regretted living a large chunk of her life without her husband, John.

These customers today, though, weren't there to chat; they were just there for free food, which they ate way too fast to enjoy the quality of, anyway. These people are used to Nutricator food, which has barely any taste. So there is really no enjoyment in eating it. With the fantastic, home-made real food sold in the diner, you need to chew slowly and enjoy every last bite. It's uncouth not to do so.Samantha glanced over to check on the kind-hearted old man she had given the pie to, just in case he needed a refill on his coffee. "Unlimited refills on coffee," was the law in Cheryl's Diner. Most places in town charged by the cup and that was for Nutricator coffee, which Samantha thought tasted like stewed sock juice.

As she looked over at his table, she saw someone was now sitting with the old man. A face she recognized, but couldn't quite place. He was a handsome man, and she remembered seeing him somewhere…

"Between the lanterns!" she suddenly exclaimed.

"Excuse me, ma'am?" A woman in a nicely cut business suit said. She had frown lines and was wearing a pair of those new SmartGlasses of which Montek was currently so proud."Oh, sorry, ma'am," Samantha apologized, then explained, "I was just thinking out loud. Can I get you anything else?"

"No," the woman curtly replied, as most people tended to do nowadays. "I've used all the free Credit Montek gave me. It was good, but I think I prefer my Nutricator's cooking."

Samantha had to stop herself from answering the woman rudely. It would be unprofessional to tell this lady her taste buds were broken if she liked that Nutri-trash food more than the real thing."Well, sweets, different strokes for different folks, as they used to say," Samantha answered with a fake smile.

Over at the table with the handsome man and the older gentleman, they were having a nice conversation.

Samantha sidled up, and politely interjected, "Why hello, sweets, fancy seeing you here. I thought we had a standing date between the lanterns. Where have you been?"

August's next word caught in his throat as he recognized that voice. He slowly turned his head and saw the beautiful Asian woman from the blackout. He could not believe his eyes or his luck. Granny's spirit had definitely directed him to this restaurant today. She was always meddling in his love life, even in the afterlife, it seemed.

"Uh, hi. Hi there. Long time no see, ma'am," August answered.

John looked at the two attractive young people and smirked knowingly, saying, "Well, how about that? Y'all know each other?"

August spluttered a little trying to find a way to answer that wouldn't embarrass him in front of this angelic woman.

Samantha beat him to it, saying, "No, sir, not really. This very kind gentleman saved me from the dark a few weeks ago when the lights went out in New Dothan for just a minute. He was as brave and gallant as a medieval knight. Weren't you, sweets?"

August's dark cheeks barely showed it, but he blushed hard and said, "Well, I wouldn't say that, ma'am. I did what anyone would have done under the circumstances. I just tried to offer some comfort and let you know everythin' would be alright. Heck, I didn't even know you were a woman when the lights went out. I was just trying to be friendly."

John shook his head and closed his eyes, then leaned in close to mockingly whisper, "Son, never tell a beautiful lady that you didn't know they was a woman. It don't really sit right with them; you catch my meanin'?"

August's face somehow grew darker.

"Oh it's alright," Samantha said, trying to make August feel more comfortable. "I didn't know I was a woman in the dark either... August, is it?"

"Yes, ma'am, it is, and this here is John," he said, motioning to the older man. "We are just about to order a feast to celebrate two important women in our lives: my granny and his wife. My treat. Ain't that right, John?"

John nodded in acknowledgment, understanding that August might just be trying to impress this lady.

Samantha looked at the state of August's work clothes, and tried real hard not to be judgmental, but being poor herself, she recognized the signs.

Before she could say anything, old John chimed in, saying, "I hope you mean Montek's treat, young man. I don't want you going even more broke on my account. I've had my pie and my coffee. I'm alright."

"No, of course, I meant Montek's treat, John," August lied. "A slip of the tongue is all. I got a lot of Credit from them today for this weird holiday, you see, ma'am."

August smiled at the gorgeous woman whom he somehow felt already madly in love with, and finally learned her name by reading her name tag.

"Sam," he said sweetly, "would you be so kind as to bring us two plates of meat loaf, two orders of green beans, and four home-made biscuits. After all that is gone, I'm havin' some chocolate pie. And maybe John will have another?"

John rubbed his calloused, old hands together in anticipation of a feast unlike any he'd had in a long time, and gleefully replied, "I can't say no to another slice of Cheryl's chocolate pie! Ooo-wee, meat loaf. REAL meat loaf. Today is my lucky day, y'all."

August and Samantha both laughed at the sweet old man's excitement. And for just a small moment in their lives, these three people experienced what it was like in Alabama in the early days; people being kind to one another — people helping one another without any expectation of reciprocation — genuine kindness from strangers.

Today's modern world was filled with too many instant gratification devices, and social media-driven interactions. No one cared to live like the old days anymore. It just took too long.

Filled with warm feelings of kindness and happiness he hadn't felt since Granny passed away, August decided to go all in here and add, "Oh, and Miss Sam, could you also please put his first slice of pie on my tab, too. I'll take care of that. I've got plenty of Credit from Montek to cover it, after all."

Samantha sure liked the sound of that. Now she wouldn't have to lie to Tara or pay out of her tips for that pie. Today was turning out to be a great day, just like John said.

"You got it, sweets," she answered. "Coming right up, you two. Y'all get back to your chat."

After the big meal, the fabulous dessert, and the wonderful conversation, John decided it was probably time to head back home to Columbus. He had work tomorrow, and he couldn't afford to miss it.

"August," he said with genuine compassion, "I truly appreciate what you did for me today, son. I know it wasn't your Credit, but you didn't have to share it with me and yet you did. In my book, that makes you a damn fine human bein'. It was a right pleasure to meet you and talk with you. I wish you nothin' but the best of luck for the rest of your life."

August, touched deeply by John's gratefulness, fought back the wetness threatening to fill his eyes. It meant the world to him to have helped this kind old man. Particularly with the bond they shared over chocolate pie and The Countdown.

"John, if I could I would have the same lunch with you every day for the rest of my life," August told him honestly. "You are a gem amongst the dirt, sir. I thank you for lettin' me sit and chat with you today."

They shook hands and exchanged a nod and a smile, and then John left the diner to make his way back to Columbus. August patted his adequately swelled belly, and gave a "hoo!" of satisfaction.

"I take it you're full, Mr. August?" Samantha asked, after saying goodbye to John as he left.

The diner had emptied out while the two men had slowly enjoyed their meal. Watching that had made Samantha euphoric; seeing them talk, laugh, and eat all of that wonderful real food bite by lovely bite. August was now the only person left in the whole diner besides Samantha and Tara.

"Yes, Sam, I would have to say that I am," he said with a sigh. "That was very likely the best meal of my entire life. Thank you so much. I'll take the bill now, or whenever you're ready."

Samantha brought over the Montek.Credit machine to his table and placed it down in front of the handsome, dark-skinned Southern gentleman. Cheryl had once told her that people used to pay with paper money. In fact, Cheryl had held out as long as she could before getting the Montek.Credit machine. It just felt impersonal, she had said. Samantha agreed, but paper money was a thing of days long gone. The only accepted form of currency, on the entire planet, was now Montek.Credit. August pulled out his cellphone and accessed his Credit app.

"A cellphone?" Samantha exclaimed. "What in the world? I haven't seen one of those since I was a kid! How can you use it? All the cell towers are long gone, I thought!"

August turned a little bit red again. People usually made fun of him for using his cell, but he just outright refused to wear a SmartChip. NO THANK YOU, SIR.

"Well, I'm a bit of a tinkerer," August muttered, not making eye contact with the beautiful woman, "and I augmented this old phone to work with the Tesla generator, and then tapped it into the Montek.Communication satellites. It's, uh, not exactly legal."

He waited for the inevitable reproach that always came with this explanation. But it never came this time.

"That is amazing, sweets!" Samantha said in awe. "I wish I had one of those. I'd take this filthy chip out of me in a heartbeat to have a cell like that."

Genuinely surprised, August looked up and locked eyes with Samantha, saying, "Well, I could make you one... if you'd like?"

"Really? It wouldn't be too much trouble?" she asked.

When he shook his head no, Samantha added, "That would be amazing, August. I'll tell you what, sweets. I don't take gifts from strangers or even handsome gentlemen with whom I'm just becoming acquainted. I'll trade you for it. I'll make you something nice in return. How long do you think it'll take you?"

"Oh, I reckon about a week to get a phone and get it all set up. Yeah, a week should do just fine," he answered.

"Ok, you come back in a week and I'll have something to trade for it. Now, let's get this Credit business done so you can get on home," she told him, gently touching his forearm.

August liked her touch and the sound of this deal. He gets something nice from her, gets to come back and see her again, and all he has to do is make her a working cell like his own. Not a bad trade at all, he thought as he began to process his Credit app with the machine.

"Oh, sweets, you're using your personal credit by accident," Samantha told him. "You should be using the free Montek.Credit, remember?"

August had been hoping she wouldn't notice. Now he had to explain, and it was going to make him seem like a liar. She'd never go out with him once she found out he'd been lying to her.

"Well, you see, uh," he began explaining with difficulty, "Montek only gave me enough Credit for a cup of coffee, Sam. But I liked John so much that I lied to him and told him I had hit the jackpot. He was hungry and sad. See, his ex-wife used to own this place. She died from The Countdown a few years ago, but he only just found out yesterday. I couldn't let him leave without eatin' his fill, you know? It wouldn't have been right."

Samantha's eyes shot wide open in surprise.

"He's THAT John? Cheryl's ex-husband?" Samantha asked, floored by the realization. "Oh my gosh. I had no idea. She used to talk about him all the time, sweets. She regretted living her life without John. That is so sad! I wish I had known who he was. I would have told him all about it. Oh, shoot."

"Well now," August said, laying a calming hand on hers. "I've got his contact information, Sam. I can pass it on to you. I'm sure he wouldn't mind. It would probably do him good to hear that she always loved him, you know? He certainly seemed to feel the same way about her."

Relief flooded into Samantha. She would be able to talk with John after all. This August seemed like one hell of a nice gentleman. Samantha was starting to hope that he would ask her out on a date.

"Yes, please if you don't mind," she told August. "I would love to talk with him about Cheryl. I just miss her so much. But don't think that I forgot about what you did," Samantha said, hands on her hips.

August realized he blew his shot with this gorgeous woman, and his heart began to recede into the solitude to which it was accustomed.

"What you did for John was the nicest gesture I've ever seen anyone do in my entire life," Samantha said, bringing August's lonely heart back into the open. "You are a good man, August; a real decent and handsome human being. I like that quite a lot, sweets. Quite a lot."

Samantha put enough flirt in there to hopefully entice August to ask her out, but not enough to seem slutty. She didn't want to come across as that kind of girl.

August smiled at the way she said it. He might have a shot at dating this beautiful woman after all. He said a silent prayer that she'd agree to go on a date with him, but he just couldn't ask right then. He was too dang nervous. August thought it would be better to wait a week, and ask when he came back with the cellphone he was going to make her.

August paid with his Credit through the machine finally, and it made the same beeping noise it always did when waiting for confirmation. The screen turned green and read, "Accepted. Credit deducted. Thank you."

Then the handheld Montek.Credit machine made a strange whirring noise and sparks flew out of it, catching August's shirt on fire. Just a little bit on fire, though.

Samantha screamed. August yelled. Tara put her hands over her mouth from behind the counter, where she had been watching the two flirt with each other. Then Samantha grabbed the coffee cup that John had left behind and doused the small fire with the remains of the old man's Folgers. It was more than she initially thought was left behind, though, and it splashed all over August's face, as well as his shirt.

August stood up faster than a bolt of lightning, embarrassed to hell and back, and quickly headed for the door.

"See you next week, sweets?" Samantha awkwardly called after him, her face grimacing in the hope he would still ask her out.

August turned back, shocked that she still wanted to see him again, and not thinking he was a doofus after seeing him on fire and covered in Folgers.

"Uh, yeah. Yeah. See you in a week… uh, sweets," he replied clumsily.

Samantha grinned and felt a flutter in her stomach. She had never felt anything like it before. It could mean only one thing… she liked him. She really liked him. No one had ever called her sweets before. That was her thing. But she liked the way it sounded when August had said it. It felt right. Samantha watched through the diner's window as he walked away.

"Today was a great day, Tara," she said wistfully. "I think I could fall in love with that man one day."

"The man you just set on fire and then threw coffee in his face?" Tara asked, laughing.

"He set himself on fire, Tara. I only put it out. I'm a damn hero," Samantha said, sticking her tongue out at her business partner and best friend.

CHAPTER 4
WEST MAIN

The next day, Samantha decided to call John and tell him how Cheryl had always felt about him. First, she accessed her SmartChip's contact list using her preprogrammed voice command "Contacts, y'all" and added his number to the very short list.

"Call John, please," she then said. As the call was being routed, she thought about the intriguing man she had met twice now. August was something special. In this modern world of instant gratification and impatience, of go go go go and no time to be slow, he was different. He had manners. He had kindness. He wasn't in a hurry to be somewhere or do something. August took his time and enjoyed the little things. And that, more so than his fine features, was what drew Samantha's thoughts to August again and again.

"He...hello," John answered, sounding in pain or at least distressed in some way.

"John? Are you ok, sweets? This is Sam. From the diner yesterday?" she said.

"Oh… hi there, ma'am. I… I'm in some great deal of pain right now," John explained. "Could we talk later maybe? I'm sorry to cut you off, but I just don't think I'll be any good in a conversation right now."

John sounded terrible, like something bad was going on for sure. Samantha intended on finding out what.

"John, where are you? What's going on?" Samantha asked. "Tell me how I can help."

"Well, dear, I'm at the clinic on West Main Street, right down from your diner, in fact. I never made it back to Columbus," John said. "A lady in a real hurry to get back to her office, Lord knows why, hit me with her AutoCar as I crossed the dang road. Funny, ain't it? I build them suckers for a livin', and now one of them's gone and killed me."

"Don't you dare talk like that, John," Samantha scolded. "I'm on my way to the clinic now to sit and visit with you. Is that ok, sweets?"

Samantha was honestly less worried about talking to him about Cheryl at this point, and more concerned about making sure John wasn't all by himself.

"I'd never dream of turning down the company of a lovely young woman like yourself. I'm in Room... 517," John told her, gasping in pain and letting out a long, uneasy breath.

"I'll be right over," she replied. "See you soon, sweets."

Samantha ended the call and then grabbed her bag before heading out the door. As she strode purposefully down West Main Street, avoiding those automatic sidewalks, and headed towards the Granger Clinic, she wished that she had August's contact information. She had forgotten to ask for it, and he never offered it up. It would be nice for him to come along to the clinic, as it seemed like he and John hit it off so well the day before.

Her head was down and not looking where she was going, lost in thought and worried about the poor old man she had only met yesterday, when she ran into something solid. Two strong hands gently gripped her shoulders and eased her back a step. Samantha gazed up into the smiling face of August, his stark, white teeth standing in such contrast to his beautifully dark skin. Looking to her left and right, she noticed they were in the same spot where they first met.

"Sam, you ok?" he asked. "I was callin' your name and thought you'd slow down or stop and notice me. But you just kept walkin'!"

Honestly, August had not minded one bit that she ran into him. She smelled like flowers and a home-cooked meal combined. It was immediately his new favorite scent.

"August, thank the Lord," Sam said with a relieved sigh. "We never traded numbers. Then I needed you but couldn't call. But, here you are. Here we are. Between the lanterns again."

August looked from side to side and noticed where they were for the first time. Strange that they should meet again in the exact same place.

"You… needed me?" He asked, his mouth turning dry. "Uh… well… I'm here now. Everythin' is gonna be ok, Sam. Just tell me what I can do."

She hadn't even told him what was wrong and this sweet man was ready to stop whatever it was he was doing to help a woman he barely knew. Samantha looked into his eyes and saw everything. She saw his heart and his soul. They were kind and warm; gentle but tough. She saw their marriage, their kids, and their grandkids… In that moment in the reflection of his eyes, she saw what could be their entire life together. And she wanted it all.

At that moment, between those two normal, everyday levitating lanterns, she realized August was her one true love. She didn't know much about him, but she just felt it in her heart and her stomach. Samantha always listened to her stomach. When it came to food or love, it didn't matter. She always listened.

"Thank you, August," she said in a daze. "Uh, well I called John; you know, from yesterday? To talk about Cheryl and all, but he was in an accident after he left the diner. He's over at the clinic right now. He says he's dying, August. I was just heading over to sit with him and keep him company. Do whatever I can for him, you know?"

August still had his hands on Samantha's shoulders. It felt right to touch her. She was warm and soft, but there was strength in those shoulders, too. She most definitely had known long days of hard work. He could feel that she wasn't just a desk jockey. She worked with her hands: he could tell by the movement of the muscles under her skin. He looked into her eyes as she talked about a man she only met yesterday. The affection and kindness that flowed out of her mouth about someone who was basically a stranger hit him hard in the gut.

Yes, this girl was beautiful. He had thought that he was in love with her the first moment he saw her between the lanterns. August realized now that it was just awe in seeing someone so visually perfect. Now, however, he felt what it surely was to fall in love. Before had felt like getting hit by a truck... Well, this felt like falling through space and time. He felt dizzy and excited. His blood felt warmer flowing through his veins, and his breath came quicker. Looking at this beautiful lady, he knew. And he knew in his heart that even if she looked like an opossum on drugs, a greasy, old trucker, or his fifth grade teacher, it wouldn't matter to him. The heart inside of her chest beat with the love and generosity that were missing from most of this world. It was everything that he had ever wanted. He had to marry this woman. He just had to. And one day he would.

All of this hit August in just an instant, and processing it for a second, he stowed it away for the time being. If John was dying, then August was going to be there for him. That old man had reminded him of how things should be. The talk they had at lunch yesterday revived August. It filled him with the desire to try and be the shining beacon of kindness that his granny had been. He owed it to John to be there for him at the end. And so he would be.

"Ok, Sam. Let's get down to the clinic," August said. "John saved my life yesterday. I wasn't dyin', but I wasn't livin' either. He reminded me of what our lives could be like; happy, friendly, takin' it slow and enjoyin' all that the world has to offer. I owe him big time."

Samantha reached up and grabbed August's hand from her shoulder and interlocked her fingers with his. They smiled at each other, and both made a silent promise that later, at some point down the line, a kiss would be very much in order. Hand-in-hand, they rushed to Granger Clinic to be with John.

They sat on opposite sides of his MediBed and listened to him tell the story again of how this had happened. August was saddened by the fact that the businesswoman had not even stopped. She was in too much of a rush to get back into the office.

At least she had called emergency services and told them what had happened.

It was a sign of the times that she wasn't even in trouble for leaving the scene. The police were supportive and understanding of the fact that she didn't want to be late to work. Unbelievable, Samantha thought.

"John, what can we get you? Are you thirsty or hungry? You want some more chocolate pie?" Sam asked, hoping to help in some way. "I can run down to the diner and grab you a slice, sweets. Heck, I'll bring the whole damn pie if you want."

John chuckled softly, winced in pain, and told her, "Naw, thank you, though, dear. I don't have much of an appetite right now. As it is, I've got all the fluids I need pumpin' into my IV. I'll be fine."

John closed his eyes, and his breathing evened out. He wasn't sleeping, just resting for a moment. August noticed that the MediBed was all messed up underneath. There were loose wires, the maglev plates were dead, and a few busted components were keeping it from sitting John up all the way. He took out the small tool kit he always carried in his back pocket and went to work.

"Whatcha' doin' down there, sweets?" Sam whispered, not wanting to disturb John. "I hope it's nothing illegal." Samantha caught August's look and winked.

"This old thing is all messed up," he replied. "I'm gonna give it a tune-up so John can be more comfortable."

John opened one eye and offered a half-hearted grin. "Thank you kindly, August," he said. "I would love to sit up a bit instead of layin' flat as a log."

While August worked away, Samantha talked with John about his ex-wife Cheryl. He told her the story of how he had spent too many nights away from home, and that she had accused him of sleeping around.

"Never happened, though," John admitted. "I only had eyes for that one lady my whole life. I was just out drinkin' and shootin' pool with my buddies. I should have been at home with her, makin' sure she was happy. It was my fault, but I was never unfaithful, though. I was only unkind and inattentive. I paid for those mistakes by losin' out on a large chunk of time with the love of my life."

Samantha's eyes ran over with tears at John's admission. It was always hard to see what you had done wrong, and then accept that you deserved the consequences. It was brave of him to be able to do so now, and he deserved to hear how Cheryl had felt about him.

"Cheryl used to talk about you all the time, John," Samantha said, her voice full of sorrow. "She said the best thing she ever did was open the diner, but the biggest mistake she ever made was leaving you. She was too proud to admit it to you,

I guess. I never asked why she left you because it was none of my business. If she had wanted to tell me, she would have. So I always assumed you had done something terrible. I never pushed her to look you up and talk it through. I…I…" She paused, fighting back sobs. "I regret that now, John. I honestly do. But you need to know that once her Countdown began, she was never sad. She worked until the last day, and Cheryl had a smile on her face the whole time. The last thing she ever said to me was:

"Y'all take care of my baby. Stick to the recipes, ya hear? Don't get all cute and try to update 'em. They are perfect as is; I promise you. And Sam, my dear, if you ever happen to fall in love… real love… don't let it go. Hold onto it tight, no matter what tries to take it from you. I let it go once, and it was a damn mistake. My only regret in this fabulous life I've led is that John isn't here to kiss me goodbye."

Silence filled the room, only to be broken by John's muted sobs. Samantha's tears were flowing freely now. It broke her heart, but she was also relieved that John now knew the truth. And John was also happy to know it.

August had stopped working and listened as Sam had recounted Cheryl's last words. He wiped his tears away, then got back to fixing up John's MediBed.

Having finished, he scooted out from under the bed and pressed a button on the armrest. The MediBed shifted and raised John up to a sitting position.

"Hey, how about that? Excellent work, August," John said, smiling now. "How in the heck did you do it?"

Now that he no longer had to lie back all the way, flat as a pancake, John felt a little better.

"It was nothin', John," August replied modestly. "Just a few loose wires soldered back into place, switched the workin' maglev plates from the bottom of the bed with the busted ones up top, and then rebooted the system. It's not 100% like brand new or nothin', but it'll get the job done."

Samantha gazed over at August and once again felt a strong connection with the handsome man. He didn't have to fix the bed. It wasn't that big of a deal, really. John's health would not have been affected either way. But August had wanted to do something nice for John. He had wanted John to be comfortable, and so went out of his way to make it happen. That selflessness was way more beautiful to Samantha than even August's genuinely caring eyes and big, strong arms, although she did rather like those, too.

John fell asleep shortly after, so August and Samantha moved out to the waiting room to give him some peace and quiet. They sat side-by-side and sipped at some awful Nutricator Cola that one of the nurses had brought them. Samantha thought it tasted like how a wet dog smells, so she politely set it down and never touched it again. August was used to it, as it was the only drink provided for free in the factory cafeteria.

"That was extraordinary, what you did in there for John's MediBed," she whispered, putting her hand on his. "Did you see how fast he conked out after you fixed it, sweets?"

"Yeah, it really was nothin', though: a simple and easy fix. What you did was amazin'," August gushed. "You gave that man closure after all these years. He finally knows that she always loved him. That is much more important that what I did. You're a special lady, you know that?"

Before Samantha could respond, Dr. Granger came into the waiting room wearing a solemn expression, and said, "Are you the two friends and/or family of Patient Hill in room 517?"

An absolutely dreadful feeling suddenly came over both August and Samantha.

"Yes, sir, we are… his friends, that is, not his family," August said fearfully. "Is somethin' the matter?"

"I'm afraid so," the doctor replied. "Would you two please follow me to my office? We'll talk in private."

They both got up in a daze and followed Dr. Granger into his private office to hear what was more than likely going to be awful news.

CHAPTER 5
THREE MINUTES

"Ok, doc, hit us with the bad news," August said, worried at how Samantha would take the news of John passing away while the two of them sat out in the waiting room. She would probably be devastated they weren't there to say goodbye and offer comfort as he died.

"Well, as you are aware," Dr. Granger stated in an emotionless monotone, "Patient Hill was struck by an AutoCar yesterday afternoon right here on West Main Street. His prognosis is not a good one, I'm afraid. It's more than likely going to be fatal. There is not much we can do for him at his age. He's got multiple breaks, internal bleeding, and some other irreversible trauma. We've been able to stabilize him thus far, but it won't continue for long, I'm sorry to say."

"Oh thank the Lord!" Samantha exclaimed. "He's not dead already. Sweets, I thought you brought us in here to give us the bad news. I was scared we wouldn't get to say goodbye."

"Yeah, me, too, Sam," August admitted, taking her hand in his. "Doc, why the hell did you lead us to believe he was dead?"

Dr. Christopher Granger blinked at them in confusion, and said flatly, "I wasn't aware that I did. I brought you two in here to show you the one and only option available to save Patient Hill."

"Why on God's green Earth do you keep calling him Patient Hill?" Samantha asked angrily. "His name is John. Call him John!"

She wasn't big on clinics. They creeped her out a little bit, and this cold, mechanical way of referring to a living, breathing human just rubbed her up the wrong way.

"It's clinic policy that we never use the Patient's first name," Dr. Granger explained. "It might lead to emotional attachments, and with the business we're in, dealing with sick and dying people… it's easier to use a formal title. I do apologize if it offends you, but such is life."

"Such is life? John is in there dyin', and you've brought us in here to tell us 'such is life'? I sure hope you have somethin' better up your sleeve than that, jack," August said, growing more agitated at this man's demeanor.

"Look, I don't know why you two are so upset," the doctor said, dropping his professional voice and adopting a more casual tone. "You barely know Patient Hill, right? It was my understanding that you only just met each other yesterday. Isn't that true?"

"Yes, sir, it is true. But he's a good and kind man, and we're upset that this is happening to him. Gosh, people today are too ok with people dyin'. Whatever happened to empathy?" August asked, growing louder and more upset.

"Calm down, sweets. Alright?" Samantha said, squeezing his hand. "Now, doc, you mentioned earlier that you wanted to talk to us about a way to save John's life?" Samantha added, prompting the doctor to change the subject. She couldn't handle the sad state of society today where death is seen as an acceptable way to ease overpopulation.

The government doesn't make citizens kill each other on TV or anything silly like that, but when someone dies, people tend to accept it and move on without a period of mourning. Samantha and August both thought it was unfair to the people who passed and the people left behind who loved them.

"Yes, yes, I did," Dr. Granger said, slipping back into his cold, professional tone. "But I don't want you to think about it as a way to save his life; it is a way to preserve his mind. Last week, Montek revealed their new division, Montek.Automaton. This new division is the next big step in robotics. They've been working for years with automated assembly lines, although the smaller components still need that human touch."

August thanked his lucky stars for that sad truth. If they used all robotic assemblies, he'd be out of a job.

"What Montek.Automaton is offering right now," the doctor continued, "is a chance to preserve the ones you love in a rather unique way. They can now download a person's mind onto what they're calling a BrainSave, and implant it into an automaton, or robot. Then the deceased Patient's family can continue to talk with them for as long as they wish. The automatons won't make any new memories, but will be able to discuss anything the Patient had in their mind at the time of their passing."

Samantha was disgusted at this revelation, and said, "That is revolting, doc. Just absolutely awful. Montek wants to suck out your memories and stick them into a cold, unfeeling robot made of wires and metal so that people can reminisce with an unemotional memory chip? That's not real. There's no love in that, sweets."

Samantha apparently did not approve. August, on the other hand, was intrigued. His primary interest was in wanting to know how the chip worked. He'd love to get a look at this BrainSave device.

"So, you're telling us the only way to save John is to put him into one of these automatons? Would it talk and act like him?" August said curiously.

51

These questions were hypothetical, of course, because August didn't have the kind of Credit this would probably require, and he was pretty sure John wouldn't want it done anyways. John was old-fashioned, and probably just wanted to go when it was his time.

"Yes, the automaton would have the same voice and vocal mannerisms as the deceased," the doctor answered. "As I said, they literally aren't meant to do much, other than hang around and talk about the past. Montek's official announcement stated that it was time people began dealing with death in a new way. Crying and mourning are a thing of the past, but being uncaring and moving on right away are affecting the culture of the planet. Their psychologists believe that, over time, we'll lose our humanity if we don't find a better way to deal with this issue. Hence Montek.Automaton." The doctor finished, spreading his arms as if revealing a brand new AutoCar.

Samantha was utterly disgusted by it all, and said, "Montek.Gross is more like it, sweets. I agree that people can't just coldly go through life letting others die without caring. But putting your loved one's memories into a damn robot is not the answer."

"I understand your position," Dr. Granger robotically intoned. "So I take it you two do not want to purchase the Montek.Automaton option for Patient Hill?"

Samantha shook her head "no" vigorously, while August posed a single question: "No, doc, we aren't. But just out of curiosity, how much does it cost?"

"It's quite affordable," the doctor replied. "Montek wants to make sure that everyone can afford it, you see. And, if the Patient agrees to have their memory switched to the Brain-Save before they die, it is significantly cheaper. This option was put in place for people, like Patient Hill, who will die regardless of what we do. We know he is going to die soon, so he can elect to switch his memory early. The process is much easier when the Patient is alive. If you were to go this route…"

Samantha had enough. She stood up and stormed out of Dr. Granger's office without another word. August had no choice but to follow quickly along behind her. He never even got to find out how much Credit it would cost for the procedure. That's ok, though. If Montek is making it, he'll probably be working on parts of this BrainSave at his factory. He can find out more about it then.

He caught up with Samantha, who was in tears as she ambled back to room 517.

"August, why?" she asked, shakily. "Why would anyone want to do that to their loved ones? It just seems… so empty and sad. When it's your time, then it's your time. You don't live artificially as an artificial person inside of a robot. It's just wrong."

53

"It's alright, Sam," he told her. "Calm down. I agree with you. It's unnatural and awful."

"Then why were you asking questions about it? It was like you were considering having that done to John," she said, her voice dripping with disappointment.

"No, ma'am. I would never," August said, taken aback. "I was just curious. In my opinion, it's really up to the person dyin' if they'd want that done to themselves. So I will tell John about it, but I have a sneakin' suspicion that he'll hate it just as much as you do."

August was right about that.

"Hell no. I ain't fixin' to be no damn android or whatever," John said with a pained look. "The good Lord is callin' me home, and I'm gonna answer. Besides, no one would want a tin can version of me that can only remember the past. I got no kids, no wife, no friends... besides you two, and that's as sad as can be since I met y'all yesterday. Nobody is gonna mourn for me, much less want to talk to me after I die."

"Oh John, I'm so sorry, sweets," Samantha said. "I wish there was something we could do. I'd give you an organ if it'd help. You and August are the only two people I've met since Cheryl died that I feel a connection with, you know?"

"Same here, old man," August agreed. "I'd give you whatever you needed if it would help. Just like Sam said, I've felt pretty alone since Granny passed away. I just can't relate to most people. They're too… distant. You and Sam feel like close friends or family, even though I just met y'all. So, don't worry about not havin' anyone who will mourn for you. We will, John. You have my word. I just wish you'd stayed in the diner one more minute... Then we coulda been friends for a long time."

"Shoot no, August. I'm already old," John said with a grin. "We'd have had three years tops."

"John, we're going to stay with you until the end. Is that alright with you, sweets?" Samantha asked quietly.

John's eyes filled with tears of appreciation and love as he looked at the two young people standing beside his bed and told them, "That would be… right kind of y'all. Right kind, indeed."

August and Samantha took turns napping while the other would keep John company. The clinic staff came in periodically to administer pain medication that would ease his passing. They were all very confused by the presence of these two young people, especially once they found out that they weren't family.

One nurse pulled Samantha aside and asked, "Why are y'all here? He got lots of Credits or something? Insurance scam? What's the deal?"

Samantha hated this nurse with all her heart until she remembered to forgive and forget, as they used to say.

"No, ma'am," she told the nurse. "He's just a friend, and I don't want him to die scared and alone."

At one point, late into the night, August was in a deep sleep, snoring softly and twitching a little now and then. John nudged Samantha on the arm and pointed over at the snoring August.

"That boy loves you, you know?" he said.

"Excuse me, sweets? We just met and barely know each other," she said, feigning offense. "But I have to admit I am rather fond of him so far."

"Baloney. You love him, too," John murmured. "I can see it when you look at each other. It's the way Cheryl and I used to look at each other in the beginnin'. I'm tellin' you now, dear: you need to hold onto that boy just like Cheryl said to you. Don't let him pull away and make the same mistake I did. Life is short, and if you mess this up, you might never get another chance at love. Real love."

Samantha looked at the sleeping man she barely knew. That flutter was in her stomach again, just like every time she thought about him. It was true that he was unlike all the other people she knew. He cared, just like she did. That had to mean something. Didn't it? Maybe John was right. Maybe she and August already did love each other.

"Maybe, John," she said, running her hands through his gray hair. "Maybe."

She continued looking at August while rubbing John's head when she felt something change.

"John? JOHN?" she yelled loudly, panic in her voice.

August shot up like a lightning bolt at the sound, and immediately ran to her side, saying, "What's goin' on, Sam?"

"John's eyes are rolled back in his head," she answered through tears, "and I think he's choking!"

Samantha didn't know what to do. She just grabbed John's hand, while August hit the emergency nurse button.

They came strolling in and checked the time. The two on-duty nurses nodded at each other and wrote some stuff down on their LightBoard, using their fingertips.

"Time of death, 2:13 AM," one of them said.

"He's not even dead yet, you horrible people!" Samantha screamed at them frantically. "He's choking! Help him! PLEASE!" Tears poured out of her eyes as she pleaded with the two uncaring nurses.

"Ma'am, please keep your voice down," the other nurse said. "Patients are sleeping in other rooms. He may not be dead now, but he will be in a minute. He can't breathe, and there's nothing we can do."

August grabbed a face mask attached to an automated breathing machine next to the bed, handed it over to the nurses and begged, "Use this. Intubate him or whatever you call it. He's a real person, damn it all! Don't let him die without trying to save him! Please!"

The nurses looked at one another and shrugged, then one said, "It won't do any good, sir. Patient Hill is a hopeless case." Then the two heartless nurses walked out of the room and back to their station.

As they did, August overheard one of them saying, "He would have been a great candidate for the new Montek.Automaton program. I wonder why they didn't buy that option, seeing as how they're so hung up on that old geezer."

John stopped struggling and breathing at 2:16 AM, a full three minutes after the two terrible nurses said he had died. August and Samantha held each other and wept until the sun came up. That's when the clinic staff asked them to leave so they could clean up the room.

CHAPTER 6
IT'S THE LAW

The two of them walked down West Main Street in a daze; both felt dizzy and lost after the events inside the clinic.

"I'll walk you home, if that's alright with you," August said, with his arm still around Sam. His thoughts were not on how pretty she was, or how marvelous it felt to hold her. His mind was on those horrible people in the clinic. How could they have let that happen? Should he and Sam have gone with the Montek.Automaton option after all? It was all too much for him to handle. So instead, he decided to focus his attention on making sure Sam got home ok and wasn't too upset. He'd do whatever it took to keep her from feeling sad for too long.

"Thank you, sweets," she sniffled, adding, "I need that right now. I don't want to be alone."

"I don't, either," he admitted shyly. August didn't mean just for now, either; he meant for the rest of his life. But he couldn't say that to her, not yet. It was way too soon.

Samantha looked up at August, correctly guessing what he had meant. She locked eyes with the beautiful stranger who felt so much more than that... so much more than someone she had just met. With what the two of them had just been through, and the losses they had both suffered in their lives due to The Countdown... Samantha felt a connection to August that she couldn't explain. When he touched her, she tingled all over. When he talked with compassion and understanding, when he cared about something... it made her feel like she was home and safe around him. He was everything she had ever hoped to find in a friend... and everything she had ever hoped to find in a lover as well.

"Do you mean that, August? Do you mean it the way I hope you mean it?" she asked quietly, looking deep into his eyes.

"I really do, Sam. You're somethin' special, and I don't want to miss out on... well, you," he answered, trying not to sound awkward. "I don't know how to explain it, but I feel like there is no one else in the entire world who feels the way I do about stuff. Everyone is so damn rushed all the time, and so worried about what's popular and what other people think. You and John are the only other people I've met since my granny died who actually... care," he said, pulling her hand up to his mouth, kissing gently on her knuckles. "Kindness is so rare these days, and I don't want to let it out of my sight for one more second. I want to hold onto it as tight as I can and never let go. I want to hold onto you, Sam."

She felt in perfect agreement with everything he was saying. She knew it was crazy, but there was a spark between them. It came from a real place, and it felt wonderful. She beamed at August, and he smiled right back.

They kissed each other standing in the middle of West Main Street. AutoCars raced by and honked their horns. The two of them didn't even notice. August held her head gently in his hands as he ran his fingers through her smooth hair. They kissed long and soft, trading secrets through their breaths. Samantha held him around the waist and rubbed at his lower back. The kiss was never-ending and eternal, yet fleeting and over way too soon.

They pulled apart and pressed their noses together, breathing heavily. August's chest heaved with excitement. He had never felt like this before. His heart beat like a drum, and he almost hummed a tune to the beat. He was ecstatic and lost in her, this beautiful woman.

Sam's legs trembled, and she held onto him for support. She had never in her life been so excited and so afraid at the same time. All she wanted was this man and nothing else. He was the sun in the center of her solar system, the gravity that held her to Earth. How could this be happening? She didn't know yet, but she was going to take Cheryl's advice. She would hold onto this feeling; she would not be left wishing August were around. She would make sure that he was always around.

August looked to the sides, and Sam followed his gaze. Somehow, they had ended up standing in between the lanterns at the end of West Main Street again; in the exact spot where they first met. It was the third time the two of them had come together here in this place, between the same two normal, everyday lanterns.

"This is my favorite spot in the entire universe, sweets," Samantha whispered to him.

"Dear Lord, it's mine, too," he replied.

–

Two months went by, and the two young people saw each other every single day. August switched his shift at the factory to match her schedule at the diner, so he could walk Samantha to work. Most days she brought home food from the diner, and they took turns eating at his place or hers. August's little apartment was becoming nicer and nicer the more he worked on it, and so he started to spend some time fixing her place up a bit, too.

They would lie on the couch or bed together for hours, telling each other every moment of their lives as far back as they could remember. They found that their lives were similar in many ways, but diverged in several as well. August had two distant and unloving parents and so got his love and caring from his granny as a child. Samantha's parents died when she was very young, and she didn't really remember them.

"What happened to them, Sam?" August asked when she revealed this painful truth.

"Well, I was too young to remember anything, but my foster parents told me it was cancer. I doubted, even back then, that they both died from cancer. So when I got a little older, I went in search of public records about them," Samantha explained. "After a lot of searching, I found them. They were both from the area of Old China; you know where Shanghai City is over in the Asian States. They apparently came to Alabama looking for jobs. The records said they were both farmers, and I read that this area was still holding onto some good farming back then. Anyway, sweets, it turns out that my father had died of cancer, but my mother... well, she committed suicide soon afterward. She jumped into Eufaula Lake with enhanced gravity rings on her ankles. The extra pull kept her down on the bottom so she couldn't come up."

"Oh no, Sam," August said, placing his hand on her own. "I'm so sorry."

"Oh, sweets, it's alright. I never knew either of them or, well, I don't remember them anyways," she replied with a tender smile. "My foster parents, Steve and Jessica, were decent enough people. They had a lovely home, and I never went without anything that I needed. They just weren't the most loving parents, you know? It's not their fault, either. Just a product of the times, I guess. The day I turned 18, they asked me to leave, as they would no longer receive any benefits from the government for keeping me. They let me keep my clothes and personal items. They even helped me to find the job at the diner and a place to live. So, all in all, they weren't completely bad. There was some good deep down in them."

"Sam, they asked to leave because they weren't gettin' paid anymore? That's just plain vile and wretched behavior," August said, disgusted. "Didn't they love you?"

"I guess they did in their own way. The way anyone today really cares about someone else: on the surface only," Samantha told him. "But I loved them. I cared for them and still do. I appreciate everything they did for me, even kicking me out. Because if they hadn't I would have never met Cheryl. The woman who taught me to cook, care, and live. She had that same spark as John, August. I wish you could have met her. She and John were very similar. I wish they could have stayed together, forever."

"Me, too, Sam. But nothing lasts forever, as they used to say," he replied.

A few days after that, Samantha was working in the diner as usual. Lunch rush had just finished, which was all of four people total, and she was tidying up. A tall and lean man walked into the diner and looked about, as if lost.

"Good afternoon, sir. Can I help you? Would you like to sit down and have something to eat? Today's special is lip-smacking good: chicken and dumplings with egg custard pie for dessert. Sweet tea included, too," Samantha said with her customary good nature and friendly smile.

"No thank you, miss. I had a Nutricator smoothie on the way over," the man replied.

Samantha rolled her eyes at the well-dressed gentleman and told him, "That ain't food, sweets. Come on, have something real for a change, won't you?"

"No, I must decline," he said flatly. "Though I wonder if you could lend me some assistance. I'm looking for Samantha Vann. Is she around, by chance?"

"Well, sweets, that's me," she answered, shocked at hearing her name out of a stranger's mouth. "Samantha Vann at your service. What's this all about, sir?"

The nice-looking man reached into his inner jacket pocket and pulled out an envelope, explaining, "This concerns the Last Will and Testament of John Hill." The man looked around at the diner, empty of patrons, and asked, "Would now be an appropriate time to discuss this with you?"

Samantha was taken even more aback, and a little lost for words. She told the man, "Well… I guess so. John's will? I thought he was more broke than the rest of us?"

The man in the suit sat down and motioned for Samantha to do the same and join him. "First, let me introduce myself," he said, offering his hand to Samantha. "My name is Lee Parr. I'm a lawyer for the state, and this whole business is rather odd and unusual. You see, you are correct. John Hill had no Credit to his name. He had very few possessions, too, only some clothes, a few cleaning items, and a bag of toiletries. That's just about it, you understand. However, as he lay in the clinic, mere minutes after arriving, he requested my services based on the recommendations of Dr. Granger. He and I play golf together once a week, you see."

"I see," Samantha said, trying to keep up.

Lee went on, saying, "Anyway, once I met with Mr. Hill he told me that he had no family and no friends… except for you and a young man named August. He didn't know your last names, he just said you two, and I quote, 'were the two nicest people I've met in many a year.' Mr. Hill then told me that he was the husband of one Cheryl Hill, owner of this diner. Now, this diner, along with her home, was left to Mr. Hill in her will once she passed away. As you are probably aware, she gave full management over to Tara White and yourself."

Sam was reeling with all of this information… Cheryl left the diner to John? She died years ago, though. He said that he just found out about her death right before he came to the diner.

"Mr. Parr, how was John the owner?" she asked. "It was my understanding that me and Tara ran the place, and kept the profits. Cheryl said that the diner was now state-owned because she owed too much Credit on it."

"Well, Miss Vann, she lied to you," Lee answered. "This diner has been owned by John Hill since Cheryl Hill passed away."

"But what about the Credit that gets automatically taken out every month? Where does that go? I thought it was paying off her debt, and that when it was all gone we'd inherit the diner. That's what she told us, Mr. Parr," Samantha said, still trying to understand.

"Well, once again she lied to you, Miss Vann. Once Mr. Hill told me his story, I verified it all with the local government and everything checks out. He never wanted the Credit or the diner, as he said it would only break his heart even more. So the Credit every month went to charity. Research for a Countdown Cure, I believe. He knew of Cheryl's death because he had to come down and sign all the paperwork when she died. He informed me that he was here to meet you. He said that before she died, Cheryl wrote him and told him about you and how you were the daughter that they never had," Lee explained. "She wanted John to take care of you with the Credit from the diner. He said that it took this long to come here and meet you because he 'was too damn scared': in his words, mind you."

Samantha needed a drink. Cheryl sent John a letter about her? And he had waited until just now to come and see everything... it all just seemed too strange for Samantha to comprehend.

"I'm following you sweets, but I'm starting to feel sick," Samantha said. "I don't know how many more surprises I can take."

"Well, here it all is laid out for you," Lee replied. "John wanted to meet you so he could give you the diner and Cheryl's house. He met you, was very pleased with how pleasant you were and was ready to sign everything over to you. Then an AutoCar struck him on West Main Street. Very unfortunate. So, I was called in, and the papers were signed. All you have to do is fill out these few forms, sign on the dotted lines, and the house and diner are yours. The payments will cease going to Countdown Cure research and go to you. That's as simple as I can make it."

"I think I'm going to faint," was Samantha's only response.

She grabbed the dirty cloth, recently used for wiping tables, and held it up to her forehead. Now was not the time to worry about some bits of food getting on her face. It was cold and wet, and that was exactly what she needed.

"Ok, Mr. Parr. I think… I think that I understand it all, I just can't believe it. You go ahead, tell me what to sign, and I'll do it," Samantha said. Looking up at the heavens and shaking her head, she added under her breath, "Cheryl, you are a sneaky old bat, but thank you, both you and John, for what y'all did for me. I love you."

Lee looked at Samantha like she had gone crazy. People didn't openly talk to the dead in Heaven anymore. Most people didn't even believe in that kind of stuff, but if they did they just kept it to themselves. He felt that this lady was obviously a bit wacko.

"Ok, madam. Just sign here and here, then fill out this portion," Lee told her.

Samantha did as instructed, and just like that she was the owner of a diner and a home. She hadn't been to Cheryl's place since she passed. Samantha loved that house. It was a three bedroom ranch over near Westgate Park: a beautiful place, and much nicer than her small apartment. But living there would mean that she and August wouldn't live close by each other anymore.

"Ok, Mr. Parr, all done," Samantha said. "Is there anything else I need to do? Where do I get the keys to the house and whatnot?"

"Well, I have the keys here. The final, formal deeds for the house and the diner will arrive in the next few days. But other than that, it's official. You are the owner of both as of this moment. Congratulations, Miss Vann," Lee said.

The possibilities opened up before her. Samantha thought of all that extra Credit she would receive, and thought of how much Credit she would save not having to buy a house. She was sincerely excited about all of it.

"I am also here on a different matter, Miss Vann," Lee added. "As I said, I work for the state, and there is a new law that just passed last week. It's part of my duties to visit all restaurants in town and let them know of this new law and make sure of their compliance. Due to an agreement with Montek, the government is now requiring all restaurants to have at least one Nutricator on the premises, so that everyone can choose to have the items on the menu cooked or created by a Nutricator."

Samantha's excitement flew out of the window in an instant. Her face grew bitter, and she said in a venomous voice, "That's not right, Mr. Parr. Neither the government nor Montek... Hell, let's be honest, we all know they're almost one and the same... but they can't tell me that I have to use their filthy, disgusting machine to feed people fake food. The whole point of places like these is that we only serve REAL food. They can't take that away from me. They just... they can't!"

Lee regarded Samantha without any emotion showing on his face and replied, "I'm sorry, Miss Vann. It's the law."

CHAPTER 7
MUSCADINE WINE

Tara fussed and fussed over the state of Samantha's hair. She put it up, then let it down, and then repeated the process all over again.

"Sam, dear, I just can't decide which way looks best on you," Tara said. "You're so damn good-looking that, either way, you'll be the most beautiful bride this town has ever seen, but I want it to be perfect for y'all. What do you think: up or down?"

"Oh sweets, it don't matter to me," Samantha said, beaming with joy. "The only thing I care about is walking down that aisle and marrying that incredible man, spending the rest of my natural-born life with him, having babies with him, and growing old together. These are the things that concern me at the moment, not my dang hair. Just put it up or down, and be quick; please and thank you."

"Yes, ma'am," Tara replied with feigned annoyance. "Jeez, Miss Bossy Pants. Get a house, a diner, and a fiancé and all of a sudden you're the queen of the world."

"Tara, I'm sorry if that came off as rude. I'm just nervous, is all," Samantha said, putting a hand on her best friend's cheek. "And you know, it all seems so sudden, even though I signed those papers for the house and our diner over a year ago, and August only proposed six months ago. Should we have waited longer?"

Samantha said "our diner" because as soon as legally possible she had signed half of it over to Tara, since she had been there just as long and worked just as hard to keep that place going.

"Do you feel like you should have waited, Sam?" Tara asked, already knowing the answer.

Samantha looked at her, and with the world's biggest smile said, "Hell no, sweets. Hell no. I want August all to myself as soon as possible; every night and day!"

Tara, still fussing with Samantha's hair, said, "Oh, tell me again how August proposed to you, Sam. I love that story."

"Well, I love it, too," Samantha replied, "So I'll tell it. As you know, I waited as long as possible to install the mandatory Nutricator in our diner. August knew I was feeling pretty upset about having it in there, so he chose that day to propose. He said that he was initially going to do it another time, but he felt that I especially needed something good to happen on that specific day, you know?"

"Mmmm-hmmm," Tara said with a grin and a wink.

Sam continued. "Anyway, as he walked me home down West Main, right as we passed between the lanterns…between our lanterns, he knelt down and pulled the box out of his pocket. As soon as he did that, I knelt down, too, and pulled a box out of my pocket."

Tara hooted with laughter at this, and said, "I utterly adore that part! Why did you have a box with a ring in it, again?"

"You see, sweets," Sam reminded her, "I was planning on asking him to marry me. I had made him a ring out of wood a couple of months before, and I'd been carrying it around just waiting for the right moment. Well, when he got down on one knee between the lanterns, I knew that was the right moment! So we asked each other at the same time right there, between the lanterns. I gave him the wooden ring I had made, and August gave me this beautiful diamond ring that used to be his granny's."

Tara and Samantha both looked at the antique ring she was wearing. It was a platinum band with an almost one-karat diamond. It wasn't big, but Samantha didn't care about that. She knew that this ring had a history, and it was important to August. It was Samantha's favorite possession.

"Sam, it's a gorgeous ring," Tara said, jealous but happy for her friend.

"Thank you, sweets. I think so, too. Now, my life is perfect except for one thing," Samantha said, sadness dripping from the words.

Tara tilted her head at Samantha, and asked, "What's that, Sam?"

Sam shook her head and closed her eyes, whispering, "Having that filthy machine in our diner, making nasty, old, fake food for silly fools who wouldn't know a good bite of food if it bit them back."

Tara threw her head back and laughed even more, saying, "Oh, it's not so bad, and you know it, Sam! Business has tripled since we put in the Nutricator. We actually make enough Credit now to afford some nice things. Did you know that last week I went ahead and got a Montek.Automaton?"

Samantha whirled on her oldest friend in the world with shock and disgust plastered all over her face and said, "Sweets, why on God's green Earth would you buy one of those dreadful things? Who is it for?"

Tara laughed at the expected response from Samantha, and replied, "It's mine, for your information. And no, I'm not dying. I just wanted to have it and be prepared, since I've already got the Credit for it. One day, I'll be standing in the corner of the diner greeting all the customers as a tin can full of memories. Won't that be just weird as all get out?"

Tara always did have a sick sense of humor. Sam said, "Then you better go before I do because I'm not having one of those things in the diner all day long. It would creep me out, sweets."

"Sam, there's at least two in the diner all the time, anyways," Tara said. "Those things have surprisingly caught on. Some people never leave home without their loved ones' memories walking beside them."

Tara was right. In the year and a half since John had passed away in the clinic on West Main Street, the Montek.Automaton had become the newest and most fashionable trend since the Nutricator. Montek's plan to soften people's hearts had worked, to a degree. People were still rude and uncaring about anyone but themselves, but now they remarkably mourned for the loss of life. Well, the loss of someone close to them at least. They still didn't care about complete strangers and their misfortunes.

The problem was, people weren't mourning and letting go. They were buying new and better models of these damned robot caskets, and taking their automatons with them everywhere. They took them to work, to dinner, to the bathroom, to church (those who still went to church, that is), to Frizball games. Name an event, and there were at least a few Montek.Automatons in attendance.

They had become so commonplace that no one even noticed anymore. If you had one with you, it was like a watch or new pair of shoes. People would compliment you on the design, and then never pay attention to it again. People's dead relatives were now relegated to an accessory.

"Be that as it may, sweets, I don't want you to be inside one of those machines. It just don't seem right to me," Sam told her long-time friend.

"Too late, Sam. I done bought one and it's gonna happen one day," Tara replied. "I don't know why you act so nasty about them. Your husband-to-be, the man you are just about to marry in a couple of minutes, is the manager of a plant that builds the automatons. That's got to be a lucrative job, right? So why hate the thing making your family lots of Credit?"

"Not at all, sweets," Sam said sourly. "Montek pays next to nothing, even for management. I've told August to quit and start a local repair shop, but he's too afraid that it would fail, and then we'd be even worse off. Hopefully, now that we'll be married, I can convince him that he doesn't need to work for Montek. I can support us while he gets the business going."

Tara nodded along, not paying much attention. She was too busy thinking about Montek's latest tech catalog that came out last week and window-shopping in her mind.

Sam kept on talking, not noticing Tara's lack of interest, saying, "I just know it would be better for us, sweets. He's obsessed with these automatons. He's neutral about if he or I should be in one when we pass, so he's not as crazy as you buying one already, but he talks about them all the time. You know, a lot of the improvements in their functions and design came from August. Of course, Montek took the credit and only paid him a small bonus, but he is the one responsible for their increased emotional capacity and dialogue options. I may not approve of those things, but I am proud of August for what he's accomplished."

"Well, I think you need to stop worrying about automatons right now," Tara said, hearing a call from outside the room. "It's time. Are you ready?"

Samantha was so nervous; her stomach was in knots. She checked the mirror and saw the gorgeous dress, her black hair down and flowing around her shoulders, and her make-up looking perfect; not too much, and not hiding her freckles, of which August was so fond.

"I'm ready, sweets," she said. "Let's do this."

-

August was a mess. His stomach was a bubbling caldron of witches' brew. He felt he might throw up, pass out, or have a very violent sit-down with the porcelain chair.

"You alright, man?" Bobby asked. "You look like terrible. Here, take a sip of this wine. It's amazing, dude."

Bobby Li had been August's only friend for as long as he could remember. He wasn't as open and caring as August would have liked in a best friend. He was like most other people today in that way. But he was fun, hilarious, could sing like an angel, and never let August down. They grew up near each other and hung out almost every day from middle school to when they graduated high school.

After that, they didn't see each other as much. August had worked on the assembly line, and Bobby was a traveling musician. He was on the road all of the time. It would be nice to say that Bobby got to travel around playing songs he wrote to huge, adoring audiences, but that was just not the case. Bobby also worked for Montek, and went to their many conventions around the country, playing soothing music that was scientifically proven to put customers in a buying mood. It was selling out big-time, but a Credit is a Credit, and you can't eat hopes and dreams.

August took the offered glass of wine. It was sweet, delicious, and had a bit of a kick to it. It was real wine. Not Nutricator garbage.

"Wow. That's fantastic, Bobbo," August said, feeling the burn in his chest. "What is it?"

"It's muscadine wine, dude. You're getting married at a muscadine vineyard, you know?" Bobby replied.

"Oh, yeah. Well, we didn't pick this place for its association with alcohol," August said. "Though now I'm thinkin' that it's a very lucky coincidence. We chose Maria's Vineyard because it's the most beautiful place for an outdoor weddin' in New Dothan. And Sam surely deserves the best."

Bobby poured another glass and handed it to August, and said, "Cheers to that, Auggie. Don't gulp it, though: I don't want you falling down when you're up there. It might embarrass your wife-to-be."

"Right. I better put this down, then," August said, resisting the temptation to down another glass of the strong wine to cool his nerves. "Oh, did you grab those things I asked about, Bobbo?"

"Yeah, man, I got 'em right here," he said, holding up the unusual bridal gift. "I still can't begin to understand why you need these, but I stopped trying to understand you and gadgets a loooooong time ago, Auggie."

The two friends shared a good, long laugh at that, and then August put one arm around Bobby and said, "Listen, Bobbo, thanks for being my best man. It means a lot to me."

"Don't get all weird on me," Bobby said, shrugging out of the hug. "We're buds, and it's my honor. Now let's get out there before she beats you to the altar."

"Right," August said, taking them from Bobby. "I need to set these up before she starts walking down the aisle."

The chairs set up for the wedding were few, but filled. They had decided on no designated sides; people could just sit wherever they wanted, and that included family. Since Samantha had no family, August had decided to skip the whole parents-sit-up-front thing. If they got there early enough, his parents could sit up front. Otherwise, they'd have to be happy with whatever they got. He had already explained this to his parents, but it didn't matter to them. By the way they reacted, August would be surprised if his parents even showed up. Which, of course, they didn't.

Looking out at the crowd, he was pleased to see two newer models of Montek.Automatons in attendance. He felt pride when he looked at those machines. After John had died, and they had the option of putting his memories inside of one of them, August had begun working on the automatons at the factory. He found that their limitations were astonishingly frustrating, and he was glad they hadn't chosen that path with John.

For starters, they couldn't have afforded it. Even a year ago when they first came out, it cost as much Credit as a new AutoCar just for the body of the automaton. Affordable, Dr. Granger had said... Yeah, right. The BrainSave was a good deal cheaper, though, and still is. The new automaton bodies were even more expensive, thanks in part to some of August's contributions. He never really thought about the ramifications of improving these machines. He just saw a problem and tried to solve it.

His surprise for Samantha in place, August stood and waited for his bride-to-be. She had not let him see the dress before the wedding. August was glad of that because now there was a sense of mystery to go along with his anticipation to marry the love of his life. Suddenly the music started, and people turned their heads, waiting to catch a glimpse of the bride.

Samantha took a deep breath and stepped out into the courtyard of the vineyard. She saw the audience turned back to look at her, and felt her face blush with embarrassment. Samantha's gaze drifted further and settled on August, who was more breathtaking than Sam had imagined. He had insisted that she not see his tuxedo or him in it. He had only done so to tease her because she had set those same rules for her dress, but now she was glad he had insisted.

She was already happier than she ever believed possible, but at seeing him in that nicely cut tux with tails and a very handsome ivory vest and tie, she was filled with even more love and anticipation. She wanted to hold him and have him hold her. She wanted to feel his heartbeat against her cheek. At that moment, Samantha never wanted to stop holding August… and then she looked above his head, and her knees went weak. The Bride began to cry tears of endless joy. Samantha didn't care if she was holding up the ceremony or making a scene. She lost control right there on the bed of roses that covered the aisle.

When Sam walked out, August's heart exploded with light. He had never seen a person looking more radiant in his life. Samantha looked more breathtaking than he had imagined possible. Her dress was a Renaissance style, and she resembled a princess from an ancient legend. It was an ivory color that matched exactly with his vest and tie. He had no idea how they had matched unintentionally, but it was perfect. It's how their entire relationship had always been: filled with fortuitous circumstance.

August could barely breathe with the sight of her looming in his vision. He noticed her look up and see the surprise he had added at the last minute. When she began to cry profoundly, August could not control himself, and he wept along with her. It was a cry that came from deep within his soul, and it was a gift to Samantha.

He didn't care if anyone judged him for crying. He didn't care if they were holding up the ceremony. It was their wedding, after all. August just wanted to hold her, and for Samantha to hold him back. He wanted to kiss the top of her head, and the back of her neck. He wanted to smell her hair and nothing else.

Samantha started walking again and then broke into a run. She collided with August in front of their gathered friends and family. She kissed him deeply to shocked gasps, and even a few oohs and ahhs.

"Are those our lanterns, sweets?" she asked breathlessly.

"The very same, love," August answered, grinning from ear to ear. "The ones from down at the end of West Main Street."

"How... how did you get them? Have you been drinking? Are you going to jail?" she asked, concealing a smile.

August laughed, and answered, "No, Sam, I'm not going to jail, but I did have a few sips of muscadine wine. Let's just say there are two perfectly good and newly repaired replacements floating above people's heads on West Main."

"It's amazing, August," Samantha said. "It's... perfect. It's us."

"I couldn't go through with this unless we had our lanterns," he said, shrugging. "Everything important that has ever happened to me happened between these lanterns. I intend to continue that tradition for the rest of our lives together. When we have babies, when we have anniversary dinners, when I hold you in our home, it'll be between the lanterns."

"I couldn't agree with you more, sweets. Now, what say we get ourselves hitched? Care to join me?" Samantha said, extending her arm for him to take.

August clicked a switch on his cell, using an app he had designed, and the two lanterns sprang to life, bathing them in the softest golden glow. From everyone watching's point of view, August and Samantha went from regular people to beings of light and magic. It was the most beautiful wedding in the history of New Dothan.

CHAPTER 8
SOMETHIN' IS BURNING

"Happy Anniversary, sweets!" Samantha squealed while handing August a large, gift-wrapped box with a big silver bow on top.

"Happy Anniversary, babe," he replied, planting a quick kiss on her soft, thin lips. "I can't believe our weddin' was a year ago, you know?" Hefting the large box in his hand, August added, "Wow, this thing feels heavy. You didn't have to get me somethin' so big, Sam!"

"Oh just hush up and open it," she urged him. "Go on."

August did as instructed and unwrapped the box. Inside, he found something that he didn't quite expect but loved nonetheless. He thought it was the coolest thing anyone had ever done for him.

"Sam, did you make this?" he asked in awe. "It's amazin', love!"

Inside the box was a carved wooden figure that stood as tall as August's knees. It was a sculpture of the newest model from the Montek.Automaton line, which was the most advanced version yet. Plus, this latest advancement was only possible because of August. Montek still didn't give out any thanks or say he was responsible. They still only gave him a small Credit bonus for all of his hard work. But August said that he didn't do it for recognition or Credit anyways. Once the man noticed something that he didn't like, August just had to find a way to fix it.

"Well, sweets. I'm just so proud of all the work you've done and how far along you've brought their odd little project, that I wanted you to have one," Samantha told her smiling husband. "And since I don't like the big tin cans, I thought this was the next-best thing. It doesn't do anything. Heck, it doesn't even have movable joints. It's just a wooden statue."

"Oh Sam," he said, turning the deceptively heavy sculpture over in his hands, "it's better than the real thing. It's a work of art, babe! I love it so much. And I love you, too. Thank you." He kissed her again, and then, rubbing his hands together, said, "Now, it's your turn!"

August took her hand and led her to the kitchen. Beside the oven was a large container. Samantha looked curiously at the box. She already had every kitchen appliance she needed.

Why would he go and buy her more?

"Well, open it, Sam," he said, now urging her on. "Don't just stand there."

Samantha walked over and tore into the box. Inside she found something revolting. Why would he do this to her? He knew how she felt about these things. It must be some sick joke. And she did not like it.

"Sweets, you know I love you… but this ain't funny. I never have and never will want one of these infernal Nutricators," she said sternly. "I cook and eat real food. You know this. Why on Earth would you buy me one?"

August patted the air with his hands to calm her down, and explained, "I know, I know, babe. But listen to me for a second. Workin' at the factory, and now being in management, we hear some things tricklin' down from on high at Montek. We were quietly informed that, just like with your diner, all homes would soon be required to have a Nutricator inside. Montek has found a way to force everyone in the world to buy their terrible machines. But… because of this they came out with a new model that is very simple and affordable, to make it easy for everyone to get one. I bought one of those, and fixed it."

"Fixed it? Like how fixed it, sweets?" she asked, now intrigued.

"I made it so that anytime you tried to use the Nutricator, it would shut down and not work for 24 hours. That way, we have one, but we'll never use it. If someone comes over and wants somethin' fake to eat, the Nutricator will seem to work and then break down. I'll tell them that I can fix it and then the next day it's back. As long as no one comes every day, or very often, and wants Nutricator food, we'll be in line with the law," he said with a proud smirk.

"Well, I can't say it's my dream present," she admitted, "but it does seem to solve an awful problem. I can't believe everyone is going to have to buy one of these dang garbage cookers. Montek has a lot of nerve. Anyways, thank you, sweets. I love you."

"Oh that's not all, babe," he said, excited to show her the next part. "I also upgraded our lanterns! First, I programmed them to be voice-activated. You can call for them from anywhere in the house, and they'll come to you. Second, they can use whatever kind of light you want now. I added different filtered colors and intensities. And last, I removed the old chips that linked them to the Tesla generator outside of town to put in ones of my design, instead. These new ones still draw power from the Tesla core, but they pull a heck of a lot more juice. If need be, we could power the whole house off of what these two lanterns can take in."

Eyes wide with surprise, she said, "Now that is something I honestly do like. Thank you, sweets. You did too much for me. I only made a janky, old, wooden robot statue."

August picked up the wooden automaton again and smiled at it, and told his wife, "Quit talkin' crazy, Sam. This is the coolest gift I've ever gotten. I love it. Now I'm gonna go start cookin' dinner. I'm thinkin' Nutricator meat loaf would be mighty fine."

He turned on the Nutricator, and it began to power up, going through its initial cycles, getting ready the processed proteins and fibers. Before it could cook anything, though, it beeped with an error message and shut down.

"Works like a charm, babe," August said with a grin. "Now, would you care to teach me how to make a REAL meat loaf?"

"Sweets," she said, already putting on her apron, "nothing would please me more."

Later that night they sat in their living room in between the lanterns, which were glowing with a soft luminescence – just enough for Sam to read a book, and for August to sketch some plans while looking at his new wooden figurine.

Suddenly, August shot up to a standing position and looked around for the source of some unseen problem.

"Sweets, is everything ok?" Samantha asked him, her heart beating fast.

"Do you smell that?" he asked quietly. "Somethin' is burning."

Samantha became even more frightened at the mention of burning, and hollered, "Oh no! The meat loaf!"

They both dashed into the kitchen, ready to do whatever it took to rescue the meat loaf, and, barring that, to save the kitchen and house if they were in jeopardy, too.

But as it turned out, everything was fine in the kitchen. The meat loaf had another fifteen minutes in the oven while the green beans and corn on the stove were simmering away ready to serve.

"Well, it's not comin' from in here," August said, sniffing the air. "I swear, though. I can smell fire. Somethin' is burning."

"I do, too, sweets," Samantha agreed. "I just can't tell where it's coming from."

They did a slow walk through the house together, looking for any bad signs: faulty wiring, smoke, fire, or anything out of the ordinary and suspicious. They found nothing unusual at all.

"Babe, I guess it's coming from outside somewhere," he said, shrugging. "Nothing to worry about."

"Maybe," Samantha agreed. "But I'm gonna look and see if it's any of the neighbors' houses."

Samantha went outside, and August went to pull the meat loaf out of the oven, as the timer had gone off.

When Samantha came back inside, the table was already set and they were ready to sit down for dinner. They took their time and savored the fabulous Southern cooking. They ate slowly to enjoy every bite of the real food made by hand.

After dinner, the happy couple went to their bedroom to get ready for sleep. They put on their nightclothes, brushed their teeth, and did a few other bedtime routines before lying down in bed to read a little more before going to sleep.

"August, I was genuinely terrified when I thought the kitchen was on fire," Samantha whispered. "Partly because I was looking forward to eating a meat loaf that we had made together, but mostly because I was scared we'd lose the house. This old house and the diner are my two favorite places on Earth. I can't stand the thought of losing, either."

"I know, love," he said, putting his hand on her bare thigh under the covers. "I don't want to think about it, either."

August moved his hand up and took hold of hers. It was warm and soft, just like the rest of his wife. He pulled their intertwined hands out of the covers and kissed her knuckles one at a time. Samantha looked into his eyes and saw a need there. The same need she felt deep within her.

They moved together gently at first, caressing each other, hands sliding under nightclothes, searching for sensitive and hot places. As they ran their hands all over each other, Samantha leaned in and licked August's lips very lightly. He opened his mouth and welcomed her kiss.

August removed her bra tank and cupped her breasts in his hands. He kissed each in turn, then reached down and yanked at her panties, desperate to get them off.

She replied in turn, tearing his boxers to remove them. Her want was as urgent as his. Their desire for each other was on a cosmic level. They each felt deep in their souls that no two people had ever lived on Earth and been so in love… and had become one so successfully.

They moved together in a pleasurable rhythm. August looked down into her face and found joy and passion within her deep, dark eyes. Samantha reached up and stroked at his chest.

"You feel so good, August," she moaned. "Don't ever stop."

August always felt a little shy when she talked during sex, so he usually just kept quiet. On the other hand, he absolutely loved it when she told him what to do. It turned him on in ways he never thought possible.

August reached down and kissed her passionately, nibbling on her lower lip as they pulled apart. They became lost in each other, time and space frozen. Their bedroom was the only light in a dark galaxy. They made incredible love between the lanterns that hovered on either side of their bed.

"I want a baby, August," she said suddenly, grabbing his face in her hands. "Give me a baby, please."

The way she said please sounded like begging, and it made August feel wanted in a way he had never felt before. "Oh God," he said at hearing the urgency in her voice.

She gripped his arms tightly as August went wild, finishing almost instantly. After a few breaths of silence, Sam moaned

in satisfaction. "Oh, I love you, sweets. That was… magnif-
icent," she said through labored breaths.

"I love you, too," he said, kissing the tip of her nose. "I mean
I'd have to be the biggest idiot in the universe not to love
someone as perfect as you are."

"You're not so bad yourself, sweets. And, God willing, we
just created a life." she sighed in return. "Our child will be so
perfect and beautiful. Boy or girl, sweets?"

"Shoot, it don't matter, Sam," he said honestly. "If it's a boy
or a girl, I'm teaching them how to fix stuff. You'll teach
them how to make stuff. We'll both teach them how to be
kind."

"You're right. If it's a boy, we'll name him John. If it's a girl,
we'll call her Cheryl. That is if you're ok with those names,"
Samantha said with a hopeful gleam in her eyes.

August held her head against his chest, his heartbeat pounding in her ear as he laughed. "Yeah, I'm good with that. But
here we are talkin' like this one time is gonna do it. We don't
know, so let's not get our hopes up."

They held each other for a long time before drifting off to
sleep. As August fell into his dreams, he could swear that he
still smelled something burning. An hour later, they were
both woken by the sound of their Home.Phone ringing.

CHAPTER 9
WHAT DO YOU CARE

Samantha wished they owned an AutoCar at that moment. Before then she had never had a desire to own one, especially after what had happened to John. They were just mindless machines that got a person to their destination without a driver, most of the time. You could take control of the wheel, but most people just got in and told the car where to go. Where was the enjoyment in that?

Samantha and August preferred to walk or ride their old-fashioned bicycles that he had fixed up for them. After finding them for sale in a scrap metal shop, he replaced the tires and brakes, buffed out the rust, painted them all nice, and put on some new seats. They were probably the only two real bicycles in all of Alabama, if not the United States of Earth.

But right now, Samantha would give anything to have an AutoCar that could get her to the diner faster.

"Oh sweets, I hope it's not bad," she said, her voice shaky with fear. "Dear Lord up above, please don't let it be bad."

August pedaled hard to keep up with Samantha. Her pace was frantic, and he was struggling to keep pace.

"Me, too, babe," he said through heavy breaths, "I'm sure... everythin' will be alright. No matter what... we'll get through it... together."

They reached out, despite the high speed of travel on their bikes, and touched hands for just a moment.

Samantha saw it first. The entire ride from the Westgate Park area down to West Main Street, they could see the smoke rising and could smell it, too. Samantha had held out hope that it was an office building across the street or a parking garage nearby. But it wasn't.

August set his kickstand right next to Sam's bike, which she had just let fall to the ground, as she covered her face with her hands and wept. He put his arms around her as he watched the Montek.Fire.Response Team work at putting out the flames that had all but decimated Cheryl's Diner to ashes.

Only two walls were still standing and the roof was long gone. The tables and chairs were almost non-existent. Samantha peeked out from behind her hands and saw that the antique ovens, stove and everything else from the kitchen were nothing but charred remnants of her life as a cook.

She fell to her knees and went even deeper into a state of loss. Her stomach felt sick, and she began to dry-heave in the grass. August knelt beside his wife and stroked her hair in the shadows formed by the dying flames, as the firefighters finally seemed to stop the fiery tempest.

Everything she had ever worked for... all gone in one stupid evening. Samantha couldn't even begin to comprehend it all. Most of the recipes were in there. Of course, she knew them by heart, but Cheryl had handwritten those cards. They weren't just recipes; they were keepsakes... they were her heirlooms. She had planned on passing them down to her great-great-great-grandchildren.

The Montek.Fire.Response chief walked over to the grieving couple and asked, "Are y'all the Lurie Family? The ones that own this diner?"

"Yessir, you called our home just a while back to let us know what was goin' on. She is half-owner of the restaurant, and her partner is Ms. Tara White," August explained, as his wife was in no fit state to carry on this conversation. "Have you called her, or will we need to do that, sir?"

The chief looked down at the highly emotional Samantha with a puzzled look on his face and said, "Ma'am, you do have Montek.Loss Insurance, right? It says here that you do."

"Yes, of course she does," August said. "I'm sorry, chief, but could you just talk to me right now, sir? She's not doin' so well, as you can see."

The chief scratched his head, still looking baffled, and added, "Well, if y'all have insurance, the place will be rebuilt in a few days. Better than before, even. Superior new walls and roof, much more fire-resistant. Probably with AutoHy-drants in the ceiling, too."

August looked up at the heavy-set man with an annoyed look plastered across his face, and said, "Yessir, and what is your point?"

"My point," the chief shouted, "is why is she so dang upset? It's all paid for!"

Samantha stood up, wiped the tears from her eyes — smear-ing soot and make-up alike — stared the chief down with a look that could scare the Devil back to Hell, and said, "Why am I upset? The woman who built this diner is dead. She was like a parent to me, sir. She gave this diner to me. It was the last real diner in New Dothan. It was the only place in town with real meat loaf, green beans, chocolate pie, and a mess of other wonderful food. Nothing you can buy down at Montek.Mart can come close to cooking that real food. Why am I so upset?"

"Yeah," he said, throwing his arms up in exasperation, "what do you care, Mrs. Lurie? It don't matter."

Samantha looked as if she was ready to fight the chief, and August was just about to pull her away, when another firefighter walked up and said, "Sir, it looks like only two things survived the fire. The Nutricator seems intact – dirty but intact. And there is a Montek.Automaton in the back that seems mostly ok."

"Thanks, Joshua," the chief said, his tone dismissing the young man. But the firefighter stood there awkwardly as if he wanted to say more, so the chief asked, "Is there anything else?"

Joshua looked at the Luries and said, "Well, there is something else…"

The chief looked impatiently at the young firefighter and motioned for him to get on with it.

"Well, sir, there is a charred skeleton next to the automaton, sir," Joshua muttered.

Samantha's heart began racing with fear. Only one person could have been in the diner after closing. And there was one of those automatons in there? Didn't Tara say she had bought one? Samantha had never seen it, probably because she had expressed such displeasure with Tara for wasting Credit on it. But why would it be at the diner? Why would she be inside with it? Did she mention something about it being delivered today?

"Sir," she said, her tone no longer angry, "I'm sorry if we have a disagreement about how I feel at the loss of the most important place to ever have been a part of my life, but you never answered my husband's question earlier. Did you call my partner, Tara?"

The chief looked from the young man over to Samantha, and nodded, saying, "We did, but there was no answer on the line provided listed in your registered emergency numbers."

Samantha rummaged through August's pockets and found his cell, quickly opened it, and looked through his contacts for Tara's number. She closed her eyes and said a little prayer before hitting the call button.

It rang three times before being picked up.

"Oh thank the heavens, she answered," Samantha said under her breath.

"I'm sorry but the Montek.Communication customer you are trying to call cannot be reached. The SmartChip attached to this account is no longer functional."

Samantha closed the cell slowly. Tears fell from her eyes once more. August had overheard the automated message and knew what it most likely meant.

"Chief," August said, "if there is nothin' more we can do I am goin' to take my wife home. Is that alright?"

The chief shrugged his shoulders as if he couldn't care any less whether Samantha and August went home or died in a fire.

"Up to y'all," he answered coldly. "Insurance man will be in touch tomorrow, I reckon."

They rode back home in silence, except for the occasional sniffle and sob from Samantha. August picked her up and carried her inside once they arrived home. He put her on the sofa and went directly to the kitchen to make Samantha a cup of her favorite tea.

She held the scalding cup in both hands and sipped gingerly at the too hot contents. August always made the tea too hot. He never remembered to add just a little cold water at the end, the way she liked it.

"It's too hot, sweets," she said, her voice thick with emotion.

"Damn," he said, slapping his head. "I forgot to add the cold water again. I'm sorry, love. I..."

He never finished the sentence as Samantha dropped the hot tea on the carpet and threw her arms around his neck. She squeezed as if her life depended on it. It hurt, but August let her go for it. She needed to let it all out, and he would let her crush the life from his body if it made her feel any better.

"Maybe it's not her, love," he whispered in Sam's ear. "Maybe it was a burglar."

"No, sweets. I have a feeling... and I trust my feelings. It's Tara," Samantha said, her voice muffled against August's shoulder. "She's gone. I just wish I knew why she was there with that damned tin can."

August stroked her hair, kissed her forehead, and said, "We should know soon. The Fire.Response Team is usually pretty fast with their investigations. Two days from now we should have some answers."

Samantha looked up, kissed her dear husband, then lay her head back against August's shoulder, and began to cry again.

"Take me to bed, won't you, sweets? I need to lie down," she murmured.

August once again gathered her light frame into his arms and walked her to their room where he lay Samantha down on her side of the bed. He kicked off his shoes and climbed in next to her. They held each other for the rest of the night, going back and forth from crying on each other, to telling stories about the diner and Tara.

The sun came up quicker than expected, and August noticed that Samantha was finally asleep. He quietly climbed out of bed and lowered the shades so she could sleep. There would be no going into work for her today, and he was going to call out, for obvious reasons. She might need him to be there for her, just in case she needed help with anything. And so he would be there.

Later that afternoon, a call came in on their Home.Phone. It was the insurance rep from Montek.Claims, who said, "Mr. Lurie, may I speak with Mrs. Lurie?"

"I'm sorry, sir. She is still asleep. It was a long night, and we didn't get much rest. She's very upset by all of this, you understand."

"Upset?" the smooth voice replied. "Oh, she won't be when she sees the payout y'all will be receiving. It's quite large. Due to the loss of the antiques, the damage to the state-of-the-art Montek.Automaton, the need for repair of the Nutricator, the loss of an employee..."

August cut him off and said sternly, "She wasn't an employee, sir. She was a business partner and a friend."

"Yes, well, be that as it may," the man replied, "she is listed on the Insurance Contract Agreement as an employee and as such will be covered that way. I've been in contact with our law division, and it seems that Ms. White had put your wife as the sole beneficiary of her belongings. So, with that and the insurance payout, you both will be receiving a check in the next couple of days with enough Credit to buy a dozen restaurants that size. You could probably both just retire on this much Credit. I'm positive of it!"

"That's fine, sir," August said, not giving a shit about the Credit. "Any word on what started the fire? And would it be possible for me to come down there and find out if there is any of the old equipment I might be able to salvage?"

"We spoke with the Montek.Fire.Response unit and they seem certain that the investigation will show that a Montek.Credit machine malfunctioned, causing the fire. And I see no problem with you going down there from our side of things, but I would check with the chief of the Fire.Response team just to be sure."

August's mind flashed back to the first time he ate in the diner. He had bought John a meal on Credit he had saved up for a new workbench. The machine had malfunctioned and sparked on him, causing August to catch fire a little bit before Sam doused him with coffee. He should have fixed it back then. If he had…

"Alright, thanks for your help, sir," August said, now feeling worse than before, despite the amount of Credit they would be receiving.

"No problem, Mr. Lurie. My name is Sidney Cobb," the man replied, "and I'll attach my number to the documents I'm forwarding you now. If you have any questions, just give me a call. We appreciate your business and congratulations on your big payday."

"Sidney, please," August begged, hoping that, for once, someone in the world could show some compassion. "My wife's best friend just died. This is not a happy time for us, do you understand?"

There was a brief pause on the line before Sidney continued, saying, "Well, I guess I can see how that would be disappointing. Maybe she activated her new BrainSave before she died. Then you could keep Ms. White around, talk to her through an automaton."

"There was a BrainSave there with the automaton?" August said hopefully. "Was it damaged?"

"No, the BrainSave was installed, so it escaped damage from the fire," Sidney explained. "You're welcome to take a look at it when you go to the diner. We'll be paying out on the Montek.Automaton, though, so I'm afraid you won't be able to take the BrainSave."

"But what if she did activate it, sir?" August asked, his heart rate soaring. "Let me take the chip, just in case! What do you care?"

"Well, I guess it can't hurt," Sidney said. "If you don't tell, I won't... you can keep the BrainSave as my way of apology for your loss."

"Ok, thank you, sir. Bye-bye," August said, disconnecting the call before Sidney could change his mind. August hoped Tara had time enough to activate that chip, for Samantha's sake at least. She may hate those automatons, but he bet she'd be glad enough at the chance to say goodbye.

CHAPTER 18
EMPTY

Samantha couldn't go to the diner again so soon. She was too distraught, and the sight of it would more than likely send her into an emotional fit again.

"Please go, sweets," she said to August. "Don't let me keep you from going. I just can't bear the thought of seeing it like that again... empty... and broken. I want you to go, though. Maybe there's something there you can bring me back that will remind me of the place... and of Cheryl ... and ...Tara." Samantha broke off, fighting off the cry, but knowing it was a battle she was soon to lose.

August gently kissed her on the lips, and then hugged her close, smelling the soot still present in her hair. She hadn't showered since coming back from the fire two nights before.

"Ok, but I won't be gone long," he whispered into her ear. "I promise."

She smiled and nodded, still not trusting her voice other than to say, "One level brighter, please and thank you," instructing the lanterns to increase their light so she could look at pictures of her and Tara together.

After a brisk ride, August pulled up to the diner on his bicycle, and the scene looked much as it did two nights before. Only now there were no firefighters with hoses coming from their trucks. The flames were long gone, but the desolation remained.

He picked his way through the debris, and looked for anything he could take back and fix up; anything at all that might make Samantha the tiniest bit happy. It was no good, though. Everything was ruined. The young firefighter had been right after all. The only two things not completely destroyed were the automaton and the Nutricator, and there was no way either of those would make her happy.

Unless Tara had activated the BrainSave, that is. Once August spotted the big machine, he rushed over to the Montek.Automaton and did a once-over visual inspection. Now that he had been put in charge of their production in the local area, he was very familiar with the construction and design of these "tin cans," as his lovely wife was so fond of calling them.

He noticed it wasn't the newest model, but it was a nice version from several types back. Some of the improvements included in this model were of his design. Not that Montek would ever give him any credit for those ideas. But as long as he and Samantha knew about it, that was all that mattered to August. He had no desire to please everyone anymore. He only wanted to help where he could and enjoy his wife's affection. That was plenty for him.

August popped open the shielded area containing the BrainSave. He couldn't check the contents here, so he placed it in his pocket and stepped carefully out of the wreckage and back to his bicycle.

Only an hour after leaving, August walked back in the front door to find Samantha asleep on the couch, holding a photo album in her lap. He grabbed a blanket and draped it over his wife, then gently guided her head down onto a pillow.

He whispered to the lanterns, "Follow, please and thank you," as he tiptoed to his workshop out back.

As he took out the BrainSave, August looked over and saw the wooden automaton statue Sam had made for him. Beside it were the blueprints for an idea he had been working on. And that idea might just come in handy now.

He placed the chip that may or may not contain the memories of Samantha's best friend off to the side, forgetting it for a while, and getting lost in the little wooden automaton project. August had a habit of getting into something deep and tuning everything else out.

He examined the wooden sculpture and his blueprints, then gathered all of the materials he would need to begin. August worked tirelessly for the next two hours while Samantha slept soundly on the couch. It was what they both needed. She desperately needed the rest to recover from the past few emotional days, and August just as badly needed to focus his mind on a task and fix something. It felt good.

The door to his workshop creaked open, and Samantha peeked her head in with a sleepy look on her face, saying, "Sweets, what are you working on? Is that the wooden sculpture I made you?"

He whirled around, surprised by her sudden appearance and made a startled gasp. Bringing a hand up to his heart as if having a heart attack, he exclaimed, "Good Lord, woman! You scared the bejeezus out of me!"

Samantha smiled genuinely for the first time since the phone rang two nights ago. There was nothing like a jump scare to make you feel better, especially when it's not you that gets scared.

"Sorry, sweets," she said, stifling a laugh. "You know that you get lost in here sometimes. Even if I knock, you won't hear me. Now, what is going on, huh?"

August held up the finished little robot and grinned at his wife and said, "I've got a surprise for you."

Setting it down on the workbench, the same old workbench he had been using for years, August connected the last of the wires in the back of the little wooden automaton. It immediately sprang to life. The wooden robot began to walk up and down the length of the workbench. After a minute or so, it just stopped and stood idle.

"What on Earth did you do to it, sweets? How is it working?" Samantha asked excitedly.

"Well, I installed a similar chip to the ones in the lanterns," he said gesturing up at them, "letting the automaton work off of the Tesla generator outside of town."

Samantha gazed up at the two lanterns they were standing between once again.

"Amazing, sweets. How is it moving, though?" she asked, leaning down to examine the newly automated figurine. "It was a solid hunk of wood earlier today!"

August picked up the surprisingly heavy robot and showed her the changes he had made and explained, "Well, I cut it. I made movable joints by adding these bolts and hinges at the shoulders, elbows, wrists, knees, etc. Then I, uh, used string."

"String? Did you say string, sweets?" she asked with a touch of doubt in her voice.

"Yeah, well it's not like yarn or nothin'. It's the same fiber coating we use to cover certain types of wires. It's real tough, it can't be cut without a plasma torch, but it moves like string. I used it to make the little guy walk and move his arms by runnin' them through this small engine I came up with."

"So it's kind of like a puppet?" she asked with a grin.

"Not really," he answered, too caught up to notice she was just messing around. "It's still an automaton. It has a few different chips that control its vision and movement."

"Can it talk, sweets?" she asked, serious this time.

"Oh, yeah. It can," August said, even more excited. "I installed an entire voice system with speakers. Little ones, of course."

Samantha took the automaton from his hands and turned it over, examining all the work he had put into modifying her creation. She was impressed. It was beautiful. So much more so than the big tin cans that people paraded through town.

"If they all looked like this, sweets, I wouldn't mind them half as much. And if they didn't have people's memories and voices inside of them, I would like them just as much as I do this one," she said with a smile, and hugged it close, adding, "Thank you, August. It's very nice. It'll be fun to watch it walk around the house, and maybe help take my mind off of... Tara."

Damn. He had forgotten about the BrainSave. August still didn't know if it had Tara's memories in it or not.

"Listen, Sam," he began, "there is a chance that Tara activated the BrainSave in her automaton before she died in the fire. If so, it will have her memories and stories, and voice, and you could talk to it... talk to her."

The look on her face went cold immediately, and Samantha said, "Sweets, you know how I feel about those damned robots. It's unnatural. It ain't right to do that to people."

"Sam, love," August said, his voice pleading, "if she activated the BrainSave, then it was her choice. It would be what she wanted. And then you would have the chance to… say goodbye."

Samantha had not fully processed the loss of her best friend until that very moment; when August said, "…Say goodbye." Sam realized that she hadn't said goodbye to Tara. The last thing she said had ever told her best friend was, "Don't forget to clean up the stove when you finish. See you tomorrow."

That wasn't a goodbye. That was instruction. It was cold and loveless. She had only really ever lost two people in her life: Cheryl and John. Cheryl had been like a mother to her for years, and when she died from the Countdown, Samantha had been there to say goodbye.

John had been Cheryl's husband, and Samantha hadn't known him that well but had heard stories about him from Cheryl. Samantha had felt a friendly connection to John at their first meeting that only blossomed into a loving admiration right up to his death. And she had got to say goodbye to him, too.

Tara, who was basically her big sister, was gone. She had died in a fire at their diner. Samantha had not been able to say goodbye to the woman who was the maid of honor at her wedding. The only person in this world, other than August, who truly cared about Sam. She had not been able to say goodbye.

Upon realizing this, Samantha crumbled into a ball on the floor and cried into the carpet. The loss she felt at that moment was equal to or greater than any she had ever felt in her entire life. Forget the diner; Samantha had her memories. Forget the antique cooking equipment; she would figure something out and make do. But Tara? Her best friend? Her "sister"?

She was gone, and Samantha had not been able to say goodbye.

And that would not do.

After a few minutes of crying on the floor while August sat with her, ready to be or do whatever she needed, Samantha suddenly sat up and said, "How does a BrainSave work, sweets?"

"Well, whenever you are ready to implant yourself into the Montek.Automaton you just press the main button, and a sharp point comes out. It seems barbaric, I know. But the instructions show you where to put it, which is right around here in the temple area, and the small spike will telescope into your mind and begin to download everything."

Samantha scrunched up her face in disgust and said, "Yuck! There isn't a better way to do it?"

"Not really, no," he admitted. "You see, once the information is removed from your mind… you die. You need to have the automaton ready to go right beside you. It will take the BrainSave once the process is over and install it right away all by itself."

"And the person just… dies?" she asked quietly.

August looked away and nodded, knowing that she was picturing Tara doing this. He knew it was an awful procedure. August realized it was against the laws of nature. But he couldn't help being fascinated by it, which especially embarrassed him.

"Yes, Sam," he answered truthfully. "They drop down about two seconds after the BrainSave is removed from their mind. They are dead before hittin' the floor. Everythin' they are or were inside the BrainSave. These new models, thanks in part to my work, have been able to capture much more than just memories and voices, though. You can have conversations. They have meanin' and understandin' now. It's so much different than when John passed away. It actually is good for those of us left behind," he said. Taking his wife's hand, he added, "As long as a person chooses to implant himself or herself into a BrainSave, I see nothing wrong with it. It's their choice, Sam."

Silence filled the workroom as Samantha held the Brain-Save, staring at it.

"And you think that this one might have Tara in it?" she asked, quiet as a mouse. "That we could put it in a tin can, and she could talk with me? I could… say goodbye?"

"Maybe," August answered with a shrug. "There are two ways to find out. I can plug it into my equipment over here and check if it contains any information. If I do that, the data may be corrupted in the process, meanin' that she might not act exactly like herself. Different kinds of glitches can occur that way. Or we can just plug the BrainSave into an automaton and… see if it works."

Samantha looked down at the little electronic chip in her hand, slightly smaller than a hockey puck, and said, "I don't want to ruin her if she is in here, so no plugging into your equipment. But how do we get an automaton? Aren't they expensive, sweets?"

"Yeah, they cost a lot these days," he said with a grin. "A good model costs as much Credit as a house. They do have some more affordable options, but I wouldn't recommend them; too many problems, which Montek knows about but doesn't care enough to fix. But, uh, we don't need an automaton, babe," he said, motioning to the automated wooden sculpture, and adding, "We already have one."

Sam looked at the knee-high wooden creation in wonder, and breathed, "Will that work, sweets?"

"I believe so," August told his wife. "I mean, it's just wood and string. It probably won't last very long, maybe a year or so, but that's more than enough time to say goodbye."

"One day is enough for me," Samantha said, making up her mind. "If it works, I only want her in there for one day. One day, you hear? Then we take it out. Ok, sweets?"

"Yes, love. We can do that," he said, taking her hands in his own.

August placed BrainSave into the port he had made on the back of the wooden automaton. There was a humming noise as the little drive inside began reading the information contained on the small black disk. He set the heavy little robot back down on the workbench, and they both waited for what seemed like forever.

The humming stopped, and there were three clicks followed by a whirring noise. The wooden robot then began walking up and down the length of the workbench, not saying a word.

"Tara, is that you? Are you in there, sweets?" Samantha said, her voice full of hope.

No answer. The automaton continued walking up and down the workbench. Tears sprang to Samantha's eyes.

"Stop, Woodrow," August said.

The automaton halted his march across the workbench.

"Damn," August whispered. "He reacted to the name I programmed for him. That means the BrainSave is… empty."

CHAPTER 11
THIS MIGHT HURT A LITTLE

Samantha looked down at the wooden automaton and scowled, saying, "Woodrow, could you please get out of the way, sweets? I'm trying to vacuum the dang carpets."

"YES," the little wooden robot replied in its strange monotone while walking in its awkward way to the opposite side of the room, directly in line to where Samantha was going to vacuum next.

"Mrs. Lurie, I have to say that is the strangest little thing I've ever seen," Lee Parr said. "It looks like a Montek.Automaton made out of wood and strings. Does it have a Brain-Save? Is there a relative in there?"

Sam smiled over at the lawyer and shook her head. "No, Mr. Parr, there isn't a BrainSave in Woodrow. It was empty, so we took it out. It's sitting over on that mantel gathering dust. My husband and I made little Woodrow. Don't mind him, though, he just walks and talks. He doesn't mean any-thing. He just keeps me company."

"It certainly is quite strange," Lee said, waving to the robot, adding, "Hello, Woodrow." The lawyer waited expectantly, staring at the odd little wooden figure, but received nothing in reply.

"Woodrow, tell the man hello, sweets," Samantha said, hands on her hips.

"HELLO SWEETS," Woodrow said, exactly as he was told to do.

Samantha threw her head back and laughed. He had never copied her like that before. The lawyer was right; Woodrow was an odd little thing.

"So, you've got some final paperwork for me to sign about Tara's property?" She asked Lee. "It took y'all long enough. She's been dead over a year now. What's been the problem?"

Lee Parr no longer worked for the state as he had when John had died years ago. He now worked exclusively for Montek, which, as everyone knew, was pretty much the same as working for the government. Six of one, half a dozen of the other, as they used to say.

"Oh, you know, Mrs. Lurie, the usual red tape," he replied. "Montek has to make sure you're not getting one Credit more than you should. But don't worry, everything has been checked and triple checked. We found no problems and your settlement is ready. I must say that after this one and the settlement you received from Montek.Claims last year, you and your husband are now quite wealthy. Why haven't you opened another diner? You could have a chain of them across the Southeast!"

Samantha looked sadly into the kitchen at the newly refurbished antique oven and stove August had bought and then fixed up for her.

"I'll cook at home, but without Tara it don't seem right to have another diner," she replied quietly.

The lawyer nodded along, not listening to Samantha or caring what she had to say, and replied, "That's nice, Mrs. Lurie. If you can just sign here, I'll be on my way again."

Samantha did as she was asked, and then walked Mr. Parr to the door with her hands on her hips. Her lower back was a little sore today. She noticed him glance back at the Brain-Save on the mantle as he left, and then to Woodrow, who was awkwardly waddling along behind them.

Finally, Mr. Parr glanced down at her belly and said, "Oh, and congratulations on your first child. How far along are you?"

"Thank you, sir," she replied, smiling and rubbing at her baby bump with one hand. "I am just now four months pregnant. So far, it ain't as easy as they would have you believe."

Mr. Parr grinned wide at her and said, "Mrs. Lurie, I was led to believe that pregnancy was actually quite difficult."

She grinned right back and told him, "Exactly what I meant, Mr. Parr. It's even harder than you heard. Now you have yourself a pleasant day. And don't come back, now, you hear? I like you and all, but we only ever see each other when someone dies. You keep far away from my door if you please."

"Yes, ma'am," he said with a tip of his hat. "But if you recall, I always bring you Credit or property. Doesn't that make it any better, Mrs. Lurie?"

"No, sir, it don't. Now get," she said with a smile and a wave before closing the door on Mr. Parr.

Woodrow pushed on the door with his little arms and said, "DON'T."

Samantha nudged him with her foot and walked back to continue the housework with one hand on her sore back. Woodrow followed right along, standing directly in the path of the vacuum again.

-

August walked the production line, observing in detail everything that was going on. He was pretty meticulous when it came to running things at the factory. Everything got done precisely and on time. However, he always had an open ear for the workers to suggest improvements in any area.

Today he was out watching how this team handled the newest model BrainSaves. One of the members of the line had told him they could improve production if they had two people on QA. There were so many BrainSaves coming down the line that one person wasn't enough. As August looked on, he had to agree that the employee had been right. They were missing a few bugged ones coming down the line, which were ending up getting packed for distribution.

He called a halt to production for just a couple of minutes so he could pull someone in to fill in temporarily until a full-time person could be trained and added to the team. With only thirty minutes until shift change, he was only putting a temporary bandage on the problem. But he wanted to make sure they all knew he was on their side, and would always try to listen to them and make changes when needed.

Phillip sat at the end of the line directly opposite from Greg, who had been doing this job since they began making Brain-Saves. Greg was giving the temp some tips on how to keep things moving along.

August signaled for the production line to start back up, and the sirens went off for six seconds beforehand to warn everyone that parts would begin moving again. Phillip was not used to the belt that brought multiple components down the line, as the section where he regularly worked required no moving belt to transport parts. Phillip had placed his hands underneath the belt mechanism as he sat down and had not moved them when the assembly line began to flow again. The scream that echoed throughout the factory shook all of the employees to their core. It was a cry full of pain and terror, and August looked on in horror as Phillip held his now handless arms in front of his face and continued to howl in agony.

"HALT PRODUCTION! NOW!" August screamed above the roar of the machinery and then jumped into action.

He gathered Phillip in his arms and raced to the factory AutoCar, which was typically used to run errands back and forth into town. He placed the mutilated worker in the back seat, and August then ripped his own shirt off to use as a tourniquet, staunching the flow of blood.

"BRING ME THE FIRST AID KIT RIGHT NOW, DAMNIT!" August screamed through the now much quieter area.

A minute or so later, someone handed the kit to August. He tore it open and found the AutoCauterizer made by Montek.Pharm. It would be painful as hell without the numbing gel provided, but he was in too much of a hurry to think of that. August gently removed his makeshift tourniquet from the ends of Phillip's arms and clicked the AutoCauterizer to ON mode.

"I'm sorry, Phil, but this might hurt a little," August said.

The tip glowed with red laser heat, and he pressed it to each gory nub in turn. Phillip's howls of pain sounded much more intense now because of August's proximity to their source.

Having sealed the wounds with laser heat, August relaxed a little. He realized this meant that Phillip's hands could not be reattached now, but August had seen what remained of those hands – chewed up by the belt as they were – and knew that they were never going to be reattached anyway. At least now Phillip wouldn't bleed to death on the way to the clinic.

"I'm sorry, Phillip. I… it's my fault for puttin' you there without the proper trainin', man," August said. "I'll get you to the clinic now. I'm sure they can provide some top-of-the-line robotic prosthetics for you. Montek will cover the costs, don't you worry. It's a work-related injury. And I'll stay with you for as long as you want. Is there someone I can call for you?"

Phillip said nothing, as he was unconscious at this point, having passed out from the pain of the AutoCauterizer. The AutoCar raced on to the clinic while August held this man in the back seat, horrified at what he had caused.

Later, August sat on the couch gulping at a glass of real beer. He had stopped at Big Guy's Pub on the way home from the clinic and picked up a growler full of the good stuff. Phillip's wife and teenage son had met them at the clinic and didn't want August to stay. They probably blamed him. He couldn't fault them for that, as he definitely blamed himself. He took another big gulp from his glass. The real beer was potent, and he wasn't used to it. After two glasses, August was already feeling the effects.

"It was all my fuckin' fault, Sam," August said with anger in his voice and tears in his eyes. "I put him there. I ruined his goddamn life with one stupid fuckin' decision. It should have been my hands mangled up by the belt. It should have been me."

Samantha reached over and held her husband's empty hand and said, "Don't talk like that, sweets. It wasn't your fault. How could you have known it would happen? Accidents happen all the time in this world. We have no control over them."

"But he wasn't trained for it, Sam!" August wailed. "He had no business bein' there! I was just tryin' to look like I was still one of them! I was tryin' to make them happy, and look what I did."

August pounded the rest of the beer in his glass and poured another. Samantha realized that he didn't need her to talk him down off the ledge right now. What he needed was for her to listen and comfort him, and so she did.

Scooting closer, she put August's head on her chest, and whispered to him, "I'm so sorry this happened, August. It must have been awful."

He put the freshly poured beer down on the table beside the couch, wrapped his arms around Samantha, and began to cry heavily. Sobs wracked throughout his body. The guilt of what his actions had caused filled August to the brim and spilled out of his eyes.

The next day he woke up when his alarm went off. August showered, shaved, and went down to make breakfast for them. The Home.Phone rang as he was frying some bacon on the stove, and had biscuits in the oven.

Samantha walked in with a smile on her face and a hand on her lower back. That lower back pain was beginning to get to her. It was always worse in the mornings. Seeing August on the phone, she kept quiet but kissed him on the cheek and took a piece of bacon from the plate of finished ones.

She watched him speaking, and saw the expression on his face change.

"Uh-huh. Yes, I understand. I can come in and give you an account of what happened," August said into the Home.Phone. "They did? I see. Ok, no problem. Thank you, sir."

August disconnected the call and flipped the bacon in the pan.

"Well, sweets, who was it?" Samantha asked.

"Work," August replied evenly. "I've been fired."

CHAPTER 12
AIN'T RIGHT

August was in a deep depression. Samantha could see it in his actions and body language. But, no matter what she tried, she just couldn't seem to cheer him up. It's not like they were in dire financial straits because he was laid off. With all the Credit they had from the two insurance settlements over the past two years, they were doing just fine. But Credit was the last thing August was worrying about, and Samantha knew it.

Filled with guilt over the accident at the factory from a few weeks ago, August still blamed himself for Phillip losing both of his hands, even though August had met with him, had seen his new robotic prostheses, and had been told point-blank that everything was fine.

The new hands were working great, and the Credit he was awarded from Workers' Compensation was enough to retire on. Montek may pay their employees peanuts, but at the first sign of trouble they throw buckets of Credit at the problem out of fear of bad press.

None of that mattered, though. August blamed himself for the accident, and there was nothing anyone could say to make him feel better.

"Sweets, I really think that we should get out of the house today," Samantha said, snuggling up next to her husband. "I'd love to go for a walk. I can make some sandwiches, and we can eat out in Solomon Park. What do you say, August? Will you be my date?"

August did smile when she called him sweets, every time – no matter what. It was the one thing in this world that still made him happy. The love of his beautiful wife, Samantha, was the glue that held his broken pieces together.

"Nothin' would make me happier, Sam," he replied. "I'll go take a shower, and be back in a few minutes."

August hadn't showered in three days, and standing under the hot spray of filtered water made his back sting, but in a good way. He stood under the steaming and cleansing rain with his hands pressed against the wall. In his mind's eye, all August could see was the red stains on the factory floor and the look of horror in Phillip's eyes. Just like every time he closed his eyes and saw this, August began to shiver uncontrollably, and tears sprang to his eyes.

August quietly uttered his new catchphrase, "It's not your fault. It's not your fault. It's not your fault."

He knew that there was nothing he could do to change what happened, and he knew that blaming himself wouldn't solve anything. August didn't want to be depressed. It's just that every time he tried to be happy, he felt it was unfair to Phillip, whose life was forever ruined, or at least altered, because of one stupid decision August had made.

August felt he could never forgive himself.

"Sweets, you almost ready?" Samantha called out. "I've got real chicken salad sandwiches and a thermos full of sweet tea all packed up and ready to go!"

When she saw him step around the corner, she felt maybe things would get better eventually. He had shaved for the first time since the accident, and he smelled wonderful. It was the cologne she loved so much, mixed with the freshly washed scent of his dark skin and beautiful skin. He had a smile on his face like the old days, and he had the lanterns floating beside him as he reached out and to embrace his wife.

"Thank you for being patient with me," he cooed into her hair. "I know it's been hard seein' me mope around, havin' a pity party. I promise you that it's over. I won't let this one accident ruin our lives. We have a family to plan for, after all."

August placed his hands on her five-month pregnant belly and kissed her gently on the lips. Samantha dropped the basket she was holding that contained their picnic lunch. She pulled him closer and turned his gentle kisses into a deep and passionate one. They began to remove each other's clothes as hastily as possible. It had been weeks since they made love last, and their bodies ached for each other in the best possible way.

Samantha could tell he was holding back, probably because of her impregnated state. She was not having any of it.

"Don't treat me like some fragile thing," she said, squeezing his biceps as hard as she could. "I won't break. Give me all you got, sweets."

August didn't need telling twice. He let loose and picked her up with both arms, placing her on the kitchen table. Samantha threw her legs open and pushed his head between them. Her moans of ecstasy filled the house as she climaxed between the lanterns.

Later, they lay on the couch holding each other and eating the chicken salad sandwiches and swigging on sweet tea to quench their thirsts.

"Well, well, well. Sweets, that was the most mind-blowing sex I've ever had in my entire life. I can barely move. You outdid yourself today, August."

She reached over and stroked his face while grinning, madly in love with the gorgeous man.

"I can't take the credit, Sam. You're amazin'. How on Earth did you do that one thing? You weren't even lookin' and…wow. I can't even explain it."

"Sweets, I attribute all my sexual prowess to my ancient Chinese heritage," Samantha said proudly. "They had an exceptional talent with sex long ago, and it must have been passed genetically to me. Or maybe... just maybe... I was aided by the ghosts of my ancestors."

"Gross," August whined with disgust. "Please don't tell me I just made love to your great-great-great-great-grandma's ghost. That would be super-nasty."

"Oh it wasn't my grandma's ghost, sweets," Samantha said reassuringly. "It was my great-great-great-great-grandpa you were fucking."

August pursed his lips, and said, "Well, that's ok, then."

They both laughed deeply and thoroughly, holding hands all the while. Everything seemed to be drifting back into place for them. Going back to normal, or as normal as it ever got in today's odd modern world.

Then the doorbell rang.

-

"I don't understand, sir," August said, utterly confused. "Why would Montek be suing us?"

"Theft and copyright infringement," the man coldly replied. "You see, recently a Montek.Law employee was in your home. Mr. Lee Parr? He reported that you had used Montek.Automaton copyrighted designs to build an automaton right here in your home. Not only that, but when your diner burnt down, you were paid for the loss of a Montek.Automaton and the BrainSave inside the unit. Mr. Parr noticed a BrainSave here in your home that looked to be... fire-damaged. Upon investigation, we discovered that the recovered automaton from the fire was missing its BrainSave. You took it and received payment for its loss, which is illegal, Mr. Lurie."

"Ok, now hold on a damn minute," August shouted, "I didn't steal designs. I created that particular model of Montek.Automaton and my wife sculpted this little guy right here out of wood, as a gift to me. Just for fun, I later automated him. It ain't hurtin' nobody."

"It makes no matter, Mr. Lurie. When you worked for the company, any creations you made or designs you came up with were and always will be the property of Montek," the well-dressed man explained. "It's in the contract agreement you signed when hired. That makes this little... thing... illegally built. We'll be seizing it immediately. You have a court date one week from today. Good day to you."

The bitter man in the fancy suit grabbed Woodrow and tossed him into a bag. Woodrow tried to get out and said, "DON'T. SWEET."

The pitiful sounds of his muffled voice from within the bag seemed like begging, but that was impossible. He didn't have the emotion chip that August had been designing. Woodrow was just wood and string. Even still, it broke Samantha's heart.

"You can't take him," she declared suddenly. "I made it as a gift for my husband. He then upgraded it for me. He is ours, and a part of our family. This ain't right, can't you see that?"

"Madam, I can see that it was wrong of you to steal and copy Montek's hard work," the bastard replied.

He then swung the bag onto the concrete walkway, breaking Woodrow into splintered pieces, just to see the devastation on August and Sam's faces. It also had the added benefit of stopping the struggling from within, which made it easier for the bastard to carry.

The man's AutoCar pulled away, and the Luries could only stare as it faded from their sight into the distance.

"Sam, are we cursed or somethin'?" August said. "Everythin' bad that can happen has happened to us. Nothin' seems to go right. I can't keep takin' hits like this, babe. What are we gonna do?"

Samantha was distraught over the loss of Woodrow, and couldn't believe that Montek, the biggest corporation the world had ever known, was wasting its time by suing them. Yes, she was sad, but Samantha was not broken. Not in the least. Sam had lost real people before, people she had loved.

"Sweets, we are blessed, not cursed," she told him, staring into his deep, caring eyes. "In this big, vast, uncaring world we found each other; two kindred spirits with a love for real life and kindness. We may have had some hurdles to jump over, and we will most likely have a lot more. But no matter what they throw at us, we will always have each other. As long as I have you… and you have me… they will never, ever break us."

August's heart felt the pain of another loss, but hearing Samantha's words helped it begin to mend. She was right, after all. Montek could take everything from them in this lawsuit, and it wouldn't matter. August and Samantha would be happy, no matter what, as long as they had each other. He put his arm around Samantha's shoulders and guided her back inside, then closed the door.

-

August, Samantha, and one of Montek's lawyers sat in a spotless and sterile room. No decorations and nothing meant to feel welcoming. Just plain white walls, a long, black table, and hard chairs that were mildly uncomfortable.

"Before we begin, would either of you like some water, Mr. and Mrs. Lurie?" the lawyer asked.

"No thank you, sir. My husband and I are just fine. We do appreciate the offer, though," Samantha replied cordially.

"Oh, it's mandatory that I ask you that," the hog-faced man said rudely. "Don't thank me. I'd rather not offer either of you a single thing."

The man had a turned-up, almost piggish nose, and the palest skin either of the Luries had ever seen. He wore his hair in a peculiar spiky fashion, and he sweat profusely despite the heavily air-conditioned state of the room.

"Mr. Tepid, there is no need for that kind of rudeness," August cut in. "We're here under pretty difficult circumstances, you know? Have a heart, buddy."

Alex Tepid looked down his pig nose at the dark-skinned man sitting in front of him. He had heard of all the wonderful improvements this man was supposed to have added to the Montek.Automaton division and didn't believe a word of it.

Mr. Tepid was from a long line of Montek.Law representatives. Both of his parents had been lawyers with the division, as had his grandparents. His lineage was Southern all the way back to the Civil War in America, which was a very, very long time ago. Somehow, despite the world now being under one government, and all nations being separate but together, his family held onto the stereotypical racism of the old South. Seeing a black man and an Asian woman married made him feel ill. Not to mention that people said this man was a genius and had made the company insane amounts of Credit through his innovations with automatons.

Alex was jealous. That was the bottom line.

"I have a heart, Mr. Lurie. I just see no reason to lie to either of you," Mr. Tepid said. "We are here because you broke the law. Twice. We demand compensation for this. Montek is willing not to press charges or to send you both to jail, under two conditions: sign back over the most recent settlement you received for the loss of your diner and employee, and Mr. Lurie must consult on a pro bono basis with the Montek.Automaton division for one year. If you agree to both of these stipulations, then all charges will be dropped."

Samantha and August looked at one another, discussing the deal with only their eyes. Samantha knew August never wanted to see that factory again after what happened there. Never mind that the company was screwing them over royally, he wouldn't really want to help them in any way, shape, or form. But the loss of that settlement was the worst. They had been making plans for that Credit.

Samantha had finally convinced August to take some time off and go see the world a little before the baby arrived. If they left next month, Sam and August could travel for at least six weeks before they would need to be back and get ready for the baby.

She had also finally got August to think about opening his own store, doing tech repairs, creating new tech, and things like that. He was so smart and so talented that he needed to be working for himself.

August had finally convinced Samantha to open another restaurant. This time, it would be a food truck, like those that were popular back in the early 2000s. It would be retro, and that would appeal to the locals. The residents of New Dothan might turn their noses up at real food not made with a Nutricator, but they were a sucker for hip and popular things. And recently, the style and music of the 2000s were becoming "cool" again. So a food truck would be an easy way to get everyone to try her cooking.

But now, with Montek demanding this settlement back, even though it was less than a drop in the bucket to the monstrous global corporation, there was no way Samantha and August could afford all of those things. They would have to choose only one. All of this passed between them in mere seconds as they looked into each other's eyes.

"That's fine, Mr. Tepid," August said.

"We agree, sir," Samantha added. "Tell us where to sign."

Alex grinned wickedly and felt like a champion. He had gotten these idiots to agree to the very first offer. He was willing to let them keep the settlement if necessary. His orders were simple: get August to work for one more year. Alex was even prepared to pay August, including a pay raise! The higher-ups said that August was close to a big breakthrough when he was foolishly fired, and they needed him to finish.

The Field Supervisor responsible for letting August go over the phone one day after the accident had mysteriously disappeared a week later. He was eventually found starved to death after accidentally locking himself inside of his own trunk in the woods with some very graphic reading materials about animals and men…together. Alex was not about to let that happen to himself. He would get what Montek wanted, no matter what. He just couldn't believe it had been this easy.

The imbeciles had signed all the necessary paperwork before Mr. Tepid let himself smile self-satisfiedly and said, "Well, that's all done with. You two can now get the hell out of here. The sight of you together makes my skin crawl. But before you go, let me ask you something… Why didn't you two negotiate? Why did you take my first offer? I thought you were supposed to be smart, August."

August reached out for Samantha's hand and squeezed it tight, then told the wretched man, "Well, Mr. Tepid, we figured that the less time we had to sit and talk with a man as closed-minded and piggish as you, the better. We don't need the Credit; we have each other. And that is worth more Credit than even Montek could ever offer us. And as far as my consultin' with Montek.Automaton? I hate to leave anythin' unfinished. I'm actually relieved they want me to come back and complete my latest project. Good day, Mr. Tepid, and God bless."

Samantha reached up and grabbed August's face to plant the biggest and wettest kiss there. They made out like a couple of teenagers right in the doorway.

Alex Tepid was visibly uncomfortable, and said, "Here, you two, stop that now. It's a disgrace. Your kind should never be allowed to be together."

"Sir, you need some love in your life," Samantha said, refusing to call this creep by her trademark, 'sweets'. "You're a lonely old pig, and you treat other people poorly, and it ain't right."

August and Samantha walked out of the room with her hand firmly planted on his butt. As they exited the building and headed towards their bicycles, August busted out laughing, and said, "I can't believe you grabbed my ass, Sam! You're hilarious. But that man was just plain terrible."

"Yep, sweets. He was the worst," Samantha agreed. "I'm glad most people don't think like that anymore. They may be cold and unkind most of the time, but at least the people of Earth don't care about things like race or sexual preference. It's enough to make a grown woman…"

Samantha didn't finish her sentence. She felt a very strange pain in her abdomen. More scared than she had ever been in her entire life, Samantha looked at August in terror, pulled his hand towards her, and said, "August, it's the baby. Something's wrong."

CHAPTER 13
IT WON'T HURT A BIT

"A placental abruption? What does that mean, doc?" August asked, looking puzzled and in disbelief. Samantha's face was in her hands, and her body was visibly shaking.

"Well, Mr. Lurie, your wife has had a miscarriage in her fifth month of pregnancy. This circumstance was due to the placenta becoming separated from her uterus," Dr. Granger explained. We're not sure why it happened. Sometimes it is from drinking or smoking during pregnancy, but according to the blood tests we ran, your wife did neither of these things."

August felt like he was in a nightmare. The edges of his vision began going black, and everything went into slow motion. The doctor was wrong. He had to be. There was no way that Samantha had a miscarriage. She was healthy; she ate REAL food. His wife walked every single day. She took vitamins. It just wasn't possible.

"But Dr. Granger, she is in her second trimester. Ain't that supposed to be the safety zone?" August asked, looking for a way to prove the doctor wrong. "Don't people say that miscarriages are only a worry in the first trimester? You should check again. She is fine, and so is the baby. Check again. Please."

Samantha continued to cry, but no so quietly anymore. August sat down next to her and held her to his chest, squeezing hard.

"Mr. Lurie, I assure there is no need to check again," the doctor said. "We've verified your wife's condition, and she has miscarried. You are correct that upon entering the second trimester the chances of having a miscarriage are low. Down to around 1% chance. But it does happen, and it has happened here with your wife. Now, we'll need to do a procedure called a D and C to remove the fetus."

"Excuse me? The fetus? You mean our baby, right? You are talkin' about our unborn child. Not just some fetus," August snapped.

"Yes, Mr. Lurie. Your baby is dead, and we need to remove it before it can cause further complications for your wife. This procedure is standard. Many pregnancies end in miscarriage, and those that end this far along will require a procedure to remove the dead fetus," Dr. Granger said, acting as if it was the most natural thing in the world.

"I wish you wouldn't use such unkind words, doc. All of this... losing our baby... it ain't an easy thing for us to deal with," August replied softly.

Dr. Granger put down the paper he was holding, and looked at August without emotion, saying, "Nonsense. It's a part of life, and you two will be ok. You can try again for another child in a year. And the procedure is simple and straightforward. You'll be sleeping in your own bed tonight, side-by-side."

August's fists balled up at his sides as he contemplated punching this "professional" for taking this tragedy too lightly. Samantha sensed her husband's anger and squeezed his arm a little. August turned around to look into his wife's dark eyes. He wiped the tears off of her cheek and stroked her straight, black hair. Then he collapsed into her lap and held her around her stomach.

Samantha wiped the rest of her tears away and cleared her throat. She regained control, looked the doctor right in his face, and said, "Ok, sweets. Let's do the procedure. I want this all over with and done. What do I need to do?"

"Just follow me in here, Patient Lurie," he replied. "We'll need to fill out a few forms, and then we can get started. It won't take long. And don't worry, it won't hurt a bit."

"Sweets," she said, fighting off more tears, "it can't hurt any worse than it already does."

Later, Samantha and August lay in their own bed, side-by-side. They held hands under the covers. All of the lights in the house were out, except for the two lanterns that hovered on either side of their bed. It was late, but neither of them cared what time it was.

They hadn't said a word since coming home. August had carried her in from the taxi, all the way to the bed. He had fixed her some sweet tea and made sure she was propped up and comfortable. He didn't cook dinner because he wasn't hungry, and he was sure that she wouldn't be able to eat a bite of food.

Samantha appreciated the fact that August had silently taken care of everything. She didn't need to hear words right now. Samantha didn't want to talk. All she needed was for him to be there.

And he was.

August had been sure to make his wife feel better, but inside he felt as if his entire life had been a trick played on him by God. His awful parents never loved him; his amazing Granny being taken away from him; meeting John and having him taken away, too; the diner being burnt down and Tara dying; the accident at the factory; the lawsuit; and now the miscarriage. The only thing that stopped him from jumping off the nearest bridge was what Samantha had said to him when he was depressed about the accident: "As long as we've got each other."

He rolled over and kissed Samantha on her cheek, snuggled up close to her, and quickly fell into a deep sleep. It had been a very long day.

Samantha watched his chest rise and fall and noticed his breathing even out into a peaceful rhythm. She thought about what she had said to him when he was depressed over the accident at his factory, "As long as we've got each other," and smiled. Then she fell into a deep sleep, too.

-

"What are you doing in here, sweets?" Samantha asked her husband.

August had been in his workshop all day. First sketching, then scavenging material from half-finished projects, and finally beginning to put something big together.

He smiled up at her and shrugged his shoulders, explaining, "I'm makin' Woodrow 2.0. Woodrow the Second. Woodrow Reborn!"

"But sweets, won't they just sue us again?" she asked warily. "I don't think I could handle that right now."

"Aha!" August exclaimed, expecting the question. "They can't sue me if I make somethin' completely different from what they're doin'. I'm startin' from scratch, basically. I'm usin' all the ideas that I had while workin' there that I never tried. I never wrote them down or told them to anyone. They

141

only ever existed in my mind. It's gonna be better than any-thin' Montek ever made," he told her with more excitement than she expected. "And I've decided that when I go to con-sult there for a year, startin' next month, I'm only gonna give them about one-third of what I would have before."

Samantha was a little worried about her man. They had both felt down ever since the D and C procedure a week ago, but August seemed frantic now; frantic in a happy kind of way, but she could tell there was more underneath, a kind of desperation.

"Ok, sweets," she told August. "It sounds wonderful. Can I do anything? I assume you'll be making him out of wood again. Can I help with that?"

August's smile spread even wider as he said, "I was hopin' you'd offer, Sam. It seems right that we make him together like we did with the last one."

Samantha wasn't sure if he meant Woodrow or the baby. August handed her a set of plans for the framework of their new wooden automaton, and he was right. This design was much different than anything Montek had ever done. It was better, too.

"It's amazing, sweets. I mean, this thing is just… incredible, August," Samantha told him, genuinely impressed.

He looked proud as a peacock, grinned at his wife, and told her, "Just wait until it's all finished, Sam. It will be a one-of-a-kind marvel."

Samantha settled herself in to do some serious woodworking. It felt wonderful to work with her hands again. Together, the couple sat in that room until the sun faded, and worked side-by-side in between the lanterns. They had never worked like this before in their lives. Feverish didn't quite describe it, but it was urgent. All of the wrongs they had experienced, all of the let-downs they had gone through, all of the tragedies they had suffered together: all of that seemed to melt away. In fact, it acted as fuel to their work, you could say.

All of the awful moments in their lives drove them to work harder, faster, and better than they ever had at anything before. Eventually, they grew too tired to continue and headed up to bed with their lanterns floating along behind them. They may have been too tired to continue creating in the workshop, but they found some additional energy once they reached the bedroom, and celebrated their love with an intense passion.

Over the next month, they worked tirelessly day and night to create this new automaton. The tiny details and engineering were left up to August while Samantha crafted the beautiful, wooden frame and multiple moving pieces. The wood they used was hard and firm. It was real wood from China, but neither of them knew what kind of tree it used to be. It was knobby and gnarled, so it took a little more time for Samantha to bend it to her will.

August realized that this new model needed to have advanced internal components, but he wanted to keep it as natural as possible. He used some metal where necessary, but most of the new automaton was wood, and in keeping with the original Woodrow he used a system of strings and pulleys to create movement in the extremities.

"Realistically, he won't last for very long," he said.

"How long do you reckon, sweets?"

Considering, August scratched at the new growth of beard on his face. He had not shaved since they began this new Woodrow.

"Honestly, I don't know. He definitely won't last as long as even the earliest Montek.Automatons, simply because of his wooden body and the string and pulley system we used, even though the mind of this new Woodrow is years ahead of anythin' that they have over at Montek."

Samantha rubbed at one of the new Woodrow's arms and said, "Sweets, I hate to tell you this now, but I kinda want him to act like the old one. I don't want a thinking, problem-solving, wooden robot. I want our little old Woodrow back."

"Yeah, I kinda figured that," August said. "He will act just like the old one, don't worry."

Samantha examined the variable components of this new version of her old, wooden companion and found something she didn't quite like.

"Is this a port to hold a BrainSave, August?" she asked.

He had known his wife would see that eventually, but was hoping it wouldn't be so soon.

"Yes, Sam. But let me explain…"

She walked out of the workshop and slammed the door, cutting off his explanation. August found her in the kitchen leaning against the counter and sipping a large glass of sweet iced tea.

"Why would you build him with a BrainSave port, August?" she said icily. "After all we have ever talked about, and after everything they have done to us. Are you considering putting yourself into an automaton? The way Montek wants everyone to do?"

"Sam, hear me out," he pleaded. "This is no corporate automaton. I built that port for either of us. If one of us goes first, this version of Woodrow will have the ability to extend one of our lives. Not as an unthinkin' robot, babe. It will be capable of so much more. And I'm not giving it to Montek. This new device is just for us."

Sam looked down at the ground, deep in thought.

"What if I don't want that, sweets?" Samantha asked. "What if, when I go, I don't want to come back in a hunk of wood?

What if, when you go, I don't want your voice coming from a lifeless shell?"

"Sam, that is your choice," he told his wife. "But if you go first, I feel like I would die without you. I would need somethin' like this so I could keep on livin'. I just know that, in my heart. But if you don't think you would, that is your decision. And if you don't wanna be put into Woodrow, that's fine. But I do want my consciousness in Woodrow if I die first. That way, if you need me, I can be there for you. Just like with Tara, when we tried to say goodbye. You don't ever have to turn it on, though."

"I just don't know, sweets. I just don't know what to think."

August took Samantha by the hands, looked deep into her soul and softly said, "Sam, you don't have to answer now. We have a long time to think about it. We might even have to build a new Woodrow before we ever have to make that decision."

She nodded slowly, then looked up and muttered, "I just hate the way those machines act. It's not real. It's just an imitation of the person who died."

"Don't think of it like these Montek.Automatons that are walking around with their prehistoric BrainSaves," he said. "That port ain't for a BrainSave, Sam. I've been workin' on a new tech for years. All up here," he said, pointing to his head. "It is completely ours and cannot be owned by Montek. I ain't built it yet, but it won't take me too long since I've been dreamin' about it for a while… Heck, I could probably make it right now with my dang eyes closed. I call it the SameSoul. This tech is so far beyond the BrainSave, babe. It will be able to capture exactly who you are or who I am at the time of death, and put that essence into Woodrow. New memories can be stored. New experiences had. New conversations. It's never been done, Sam."

"I don't know, sweets. It sounds… sacrilegious," she said in a quiet voice. "You can't hold someone's soul from going to Heaven or Hell."

"Well, I like to think that it's not your whole soul in there. It would just be a tiny part, meant to let the other one of us say goodbye in our own time. Like I said, it won't last forever anyways," August replied.

"But what if it hurts to be inside of that thing? What if it's actually eternal agony, but we can't express it, sweets?"

She pulled August close and held her head against his chest, breathing in the aroma of his hard work, and noticing she had her own pungent smell to match.

"Sam, don't worry," he reassured her. "It won't hurt a bit."

CHAPTER 14
HELPFUL BUT AWKWARD

"Woodrow, please move this shelvin' unit to that wall," August instructed the tall, wooden automaton.

"SHELL VING," Woodrow replied.

Having an unthinking automaton to help you set up your new business can be quite handy, as August was finding out. Over the past year, Samantha and August had found multiple uses for the new Woodrow and his new size. No longer a small thing, standing 5'10", he was capable of a lot more and turned out to be a great help around the house.

Watching the two at work, Sam was ecstatic. She felt that August had finally come to his senses by starting his own tech shop, which he called Sweets, Inc., naturally. She even had no problem doing all the housework for a while, so that Woodrow could help set up the new shop.

"You two could use a break, sweets," she said to August. "You've been at it for hours."

August glanced back and wiped the sweat from his brow, smiling at his wife.

"I sure could," he answered, "but I don't think Woodrow is even winded."

"WIN DID," the helpful but awkward robot replied.

The married couple laughed at their strange wooden friend. The neighbors had been thoroughly shocked when they first saw Woodrow. He looked nothing like the boxy, inhuman Montek.Automatons. He had a very human-like body shape, carved out lovingly by Samantha. There were grooves where the tough-fibered and almost unbreakable strings of tubing ran along his arms and legs going into his mid-section, which housed the motor that controlled Woodrow's movements. He hummed slightly and made sounds like children's building blocks clacking together when he walked.

Now, though, the entire neighborhood was used to seeing the sleek wooden robot. Montek had heard about Woodrow and had sent their lawyers around with some techs from the Montek.Automaton division. They found absolutely nothing in common with their property, so they could not say a thing about this new Woodrow.

August had completed his mandatory free year of consultation, and, as he had promised his wife, had only given them just enough information to satisfy the higher-ups, making no innovations during his time back in their grasp, and creating nothing close to Woodrow 2.0. When they finally did see this new automaton, the Montek officials scoffed at the material used to build him. But upon inspecting his internal components, the Montek employees were impressed to the point of jealousy and suspicion.

"Why didn't you use this technology, or even tell us about it while consulting for Montek?" one of the lawyers had asked.

"It's just something I've been messing around with in my home workshop. I didn't think Montek would be interested in this kind of tech," August had answered.

Now that his time with them was over, and Sweets, Inc was close to opening., August was ecstatic. His shop would specialize in tech repair, but also offer his own line of affordable products to solve modern problems. He, of course, offered nothing made by Montek. Every piece of tech in the shop was of August's personal design.

August had created a line of levitating lanterns, modeled after the modifications he had made to his and Sam's lanterns. He had a line of cellphones for people who didn't want to use a SmartChip. August figured the target audience was small for that, but people did love retro stuff these days, so maybe it would be a big seller. Time would tell. He couldn't use his cellphone's design, tapping into Montek.Communication satellites, since it was illegal. Instead, he modded old cellphones and even built new ones from scratch that could hold a SmartChip inside. People would still have to pay Montek.Communication for their bills; they just wouldn't have a chip implanted in their ear anymore.

He also had an oven that was easier to use than the real one he and Sam had at home. It was automated, which people would like. But it required the use of real ingredients and food. No Nutricator muck put into a reservoir in the back. Samantha was especially hoping this one would be a big seller.

"Well, sweets, come on over here and have some lunch," his wife said. "I made your favorite: meat loaf, green beans, and home-made biscuits. There's sweet tea to drink, too."

August came over and sat down on the blanket Sam had laid out for them. As he hungrily devoured the delicious food she had made for them, he took it all in. His shop was fantastic. He was as proud of this as he was of Woodrow. August believed that it would be successful in this neighborhood. Of course, they had rented a spot on West Main Street, very close to where they had first met.

Samantha looked around and took it all in. She was so impressed by how much August had accomplished since their first meeting. He had gone from an awkward tinkerer working on an assembly line in a factory to an inventor that held a lot of clout with the biggest corporation and seller of tech in the entire world. Just a regular guy from Alabama had made a real mark in the major company on Earth.

"When are you going to open the shop, sweets?" she asked, her voice tight with emotion.

August shrugged his shoulders, chewed on a biscuit, and said, "Everythin' is almost ready to go. I figure I can put out some flyers, maybe an ad in the New Dothan Eagle digital news, you know, let people know about us. Maybe offer some Grand Openin' discounts? People love a good deal."

Samantha ran her fingers lightly across his thigh and said, "I actually had an idea about the logo and slogan. I thought that since a lot of people were into retro stuff, and since a lot of your tech plays off of that, we could play on that idea. Something like, 'Yesterday's Answers to Tomorrow's Problems' and have a picture of you with a cellphone up to your ear and me cooking on one of your new ovens. What do you think of that, sweets?"

August rubbed his lightly bearded face and looked sternly at the floor, before shaking his head in disagreement.

"I don't like it, babe. Nope, I don't like it," he said in a disapproving voice. "I LOVE IT!" he then yelled to the ceiling.

August grabbed her in a constricting embrace and they rolled around on the newly installed gel-cushioned floors, which made for a nice place to stand on your feet all day, but also an excellent place to mess around when the time was right. And the time was suddenly right.

–

"Hi! Welcome to Sweets, Inc. We have yesterday's answers to tomorrow's problems. Are you lookin' for anythin' in particular today?" August said, greeting the new customer the same way he greeted everyone who came into his store.

His first week of business had so far been incredible. Everyone in the area had to come in to see what this new store was all about. And the desire to be the first one of your friends with the newest gadget had certainly helped business.

"Well, normally I would say that I was just browsing, but I have to be honest with you," the man said. "My cousin told me he bought one of your cellphones and a set of your lanterns. The way he described them made me want to come and have a look for myself. Can you show me what he was talking about?"

August had to grin. Those had been the two most popular items since he had opened. It was funny to him because one was an old version of new tech: the cellphone. But the other was a new version of old tech: the lanterns. And for whatever reason, those two are what the people wanted.

There was some repair work coming in, too. People came to see August because he would fix and mod any tech; not just his stuff, but also Montek's and other companies' products. His competition would only ever touch their own products.

"Absolutely, sir," August cheerily replied. "Over here we have all the available models of our Sweet Phones. As I'm sure your cousin told you, we take an existin' SmartChip and insert it into any one of these you'd like. It's not a replacement for a SmartChip, you understand? Just an accessory that gets that tech out of your head and into your hand. It's a little bit like takin' a step back in time. You'll have the same functions as you do now, you'll just look more… old school, as they used to say."

The customer was visibly interested but said nothing. August could just tell by his body language that the guy was going to buy one.

"Over here we have the Life Lanterns," August continued. "A while back, I bought some of the city's maglev lanterns that you see on every street. My wife and I had some very personal moments between those lanterns and I wanted to have them in our home as a symbol of our life together. I modded them out with voice recognition software, multiple light filters, a dimming feature, and a simple AI; they'll follow you when told to do so, or stay put when instructed. You can voice command all of it, or tell the lanterns to enter predictive mode and assume what you want based on past instructions. They can learn your habits, sir!"

At this, the customer couldn't stay quiet anymore. August could tell: the man just had to have this stuff.

"Ok, I don't care what they cost," the customer said greed-ily. "I need two sets of Life Lanterns and two Sweet Phones. Ring it up."

As August began to type up the order and enter it into the system, Woodrow walked onto the sales floor from the back room.

"Whoa," the customer exclaimed, "what on Earth is that thing?"

August laughed a little and gestured to Woodrow with an air of theatrics.

"That, my friend," he said, "is my pride and joy. Made by my wife and me workin' together. It's a wooden automaton, with the most sophisticated internal components the world has ever seen. Woodrow is the only employee I'll ever need, and a major part of our family. He's pretty helpful, but a little awkward. Ain't that right, Woodrow?"

"RIGHT," the wooden robot replied.

The customer stroked his chin and squinted his eyes as he assessed as this new tech was strolling across the floor. Woodrow wandered over to a display of Life Lanterns, straightened it, and then went back into the stockroom.

"Now that is something I'd be interested in buying! How much for one of those wooden automatons? It's like the fu-ture and the past all mixed into one. I've never seen anything like it!"

August just shook his head and smiled apologetically, saying, "I'm terribly sorry, sir, but Woodrow is one of a kind and will stay that way. He's a special part of our family. My wife and I made him, and we certainly don't want a bunch of copies runnin' around. I'm very sorry."

The customer looked disappointed, but not upset. August could tell the man wasn't ready to give up just yet. Already, quite a few residents of New Dothan had begged to buy Woodrow, or even have August make a duplicate. With the popular fashion right now being retro, people went crazy over the wooden but sophisticated automaton.

"Oh, it's alright, Mr. Lurie. I totally understand. He does seem to appropriately be one of a kind," the customer replied. "Thank you for the phones and lanterns. I'm sure I'll be back soon. This is a fabulous shop with some truly unique tech. Goodbye, now."

"Thank you for your business, sir. We hope to see you soon. Tell your friends about us!" August said, waving goodbye.

The man walked out of the shop with his purchases, and Woodrow came back onto the floor to refill the phone and lantern displays. August replayed the interaction with the man over in his head for a minute. There was something a little bit funny about him, but August couldn't put his finger on it.

Looking at the receipt, August noticed the customer's name, Joshua Stevens. August had never heard the name before. But there was something odd about him. For one, the man was rather pleasant. That was relatively unusual; most people were brusque and ill-mannered. This Joshua fellow was complimentary and even said goodbye. Most folks just bought something and left, only saying how cool everyone would think they were now that they had this weird tech.

August didn't want to judge the man negatively for having manners, but it was unusual. For the most part, the only people he had ever known with a lick of manners was his wife, his granny, John from the diner, and even Tara and Bobby, to a degree.

But that wasn't even all of it. There was something else strange about the encounter. What was ringing alarm bells in August's head?

Suddenly, it hit him.

"He called me Mr. Lurie, Woodrow, but I never told him my name. Strange."

CHAPTER 15
PATIENT LURIE

The clinic on West Main Street was pretty much the same as the day John had died there years ago, and only a few months ago when August and Samantha had been there for the miscarriage.

It looked the same. It smelled the same. The same nurses worked there with their same cold stares. Dr. Granger still ran things with a feeling of checking things off of a list rather than making patients feel at ease.

But somehow, it felt much scarier today.

Dr. Granger straightened some paperwork on his desk and began asking questions without actually seeming to care what the answers were.

"So, Patient Lurie," he said, "it says here that you have been experiencing what you thought were panic attacks. Then a week ago they turned into headaches. Is that correct?"

Patient Lurie only nodded, feeling too afraid to do anything else.

"And your bowel movements have become infrequent, but painful and loose when you do have them. Is this also correct?" the doctor asked.

Again, only a nod in reply to the cold doctor, fear leaving the patient unable to speak.

"Ok. Well, what I'd like to do is order some blood work and a few scans," Dr. Granger said. "It sounds bad, but you never know until you check. So, for now, I'd like you to follow the nurse, and he'll do the necessary procedures."

Patient Lurie nodded again and stared at the floor. Things had been going so well lately. The shop was doing amazing. The whole city lusted after the inventions found at Sweets, Inc. They could barely keep up with demand.

The Lurie family was doing incredibly well financially, in fact, because of the shop's instant success. They had even heard rumors that the local Montek.Mart's tech department was trending down from last year's sales because of Sweets, Inc. That was huge.

Montek, the biggest company on Earth, was suffering sales losses in one tiny city due to one little start-up tech company. Insignificant news to Montek for sure, but it was humongous news to the young start-up company.

That was all Patient Lurie could think about right now. With all the hardships and obstacles they had overcome together through the years, August and Samantha had finally come out on top. They were finally saving enough Credit to go on a tour of the world. They would finally be able to travel and see everything. And then the panic attacks, headaches, and other symptoms had shown up. Patient Lurie had a bad feeling about them, and that is what brought about the visit to Dr. Granger's clinic on West Main Street.

A secret visit to be sure, though. What if it was nothing? What if it was just the stress of having a family-run small business? What if it was just the flu? No, it was better to come in secret and have some tests done just in case it turned out to be nothing at all.

"Patient Lurie?" a familiar-looking man said. "Follow me. Quit staring into space and get up."

Dozens of pinpricks, a few scans, and a mouth scrape later, Patient Lurie sat alone in a waiting room. What to do now? Go home? Go to the shop? The whole ordeal had only taken an hour at best. The rest of the day was wide open, but how to enjoy any of it?

While Patient Lurie was pondering this, Dr. Granger strode into the room and sat down in the chair directly opposite the worried patient.

"It's cancer," he said as if ordering toast. "You have cancer. A very aggressive form."

Patient Lurie began to cry silently, tears running down cheeks already red with worry.

"Oh stop crying," Dr. Granger said, rolling his eyes. "We have a cure for cancer. It's no problem. You'll take this pill, and then you're cured. Then you'll have to take these other pills for two weeks to fix the damage already done to your organs. But you'll be fine."

Patient Lurie cried even harder now. But these were tears of relief. When the doctor had said cancer, the only thought that registered was... The Countdown. It couldn't be normal cancer, of course, because the Luries weren't so lucky as that. But thank God, it was just regular old curable cancer, and nothing to worry about.

"Here take this prescription to the front and one of the nurses will tell you everything you need to do and get your Credit," the doctor said, dismissing the patient. "Oh, and, uh, congratulations on being able to keep living," he added. Obviously, Dr. Granger was trying to improve his bedside manner.

Patient Lurie wanted to hit the good doctor but refrained from doing so. It wouldn't solve anything. Plus, it was time to celebrate... not go to jail for assault.

At the front desk, the two nurses were using an app called Montek.Bets, a simple way to exchange Credit from person to person quickly. It was nothing more than the privatization of gambling. There were limits set on the app so that people could only place small bets. It wouldn't allow the exchange of large sums of Credit.

"I told you, man. No way was it The Countdown," one of the cretins said. "We've already had a bunch of people this month start their Countdown. I knew this patient wouldn't be one of them."

"Screw you, man. Patient Lurie seemed like a perfect candidate for The Countdown. You just got lucky," the other nurse replied.

"Unbelievable," Patient Lurie mumbled.

They were betting on whether it was a terminal disease or a curable one, and they didn't even have the decency to talk about it in private. Just blabbing their emotionless, uncaring, fat mouths right there at the front desk. It was disgusting, but nothing to worry about.

Regular curable cancer was great news, so Patient Lurie used the Montek.Credit machine and paid the fee before rushing out onto West Main Street and letting loose the biggest celebratory yell that New Dothan had heard in years.

People riding the automated sidewalks on either side of the street stared with looks of confusion or disgust. Patient Lurie didn't give a damn.

CHAPTER 16
WHAT THE HELL

The shop had only been open for six months before August and Samantha closed for a week-long vacation. The amount of business coming through their doors was amazing. Repeat customers, referred customers, walk-ins, and customers with coupons from the New Dothan Eagle digital newspaper.

They had banked so much profit in those first six months that closing up shop for a week and flying down to the island of Jamaica City was no problem at all. August had left Woodrow in the workshop to fill orders and act as security while they were gone. He was such a great help, but August was worried about using the wooden automaton too much. Woodrow was starting to show some serious wear and tear already. Pretty soon Samantha and August would have to craft a few replacement parts; nothing vital yet, but still necessary to keep him going.

Lounging in beach chairs under the shade of a large tree while listening to the nearby roll and crash of the waves, the two lovers sipped their fruity drinks and sighed in unison.

"We should just move here, sweets," Samantha said lazily. "I don't ever want to go back to New Dothan."

August let loose a sudden guffaw, causing his wife to spill some boozy red cocktail down the front of her bikini.

"Oh, sorry, honey," he apologized, wiping at the spilled drink with his bare hands, and licking it off his fingers. "I don't think we can afford to live here full-time just yet, though, Sam. Maybe in a few years."

Samantha wiped more of the drink from between her breasts and flung it at her husband, and said, "Well maybe we could just move the whole shop here, sweets. People in Jamaica City would love your inventions, too. We don't need to be wealthy; we just need to be happy."

August reached out, grasped her hand, and said, "I am happy, Sam: very, very happy." He paused, bringing her hand to his lips, kissed her knuckles gently, then added, "I love you more than you know."

Samantha lowered her sunglasses, looking over them at the love of her life, and replied, "If you're happy in New Dothan, just imagine how happy you'd be here. And don't think for one second that you love me any more than I love you, mister. I love you more than there are stars in the sky."

"Oh yeah, babe? Well, I love you more than there are grains of sand on every beach on every planet in this and all other universes. Beat that," he said, still clutching her hand.

"Oh shut up, you old softy," Samantha said, leaning forward to kiss her husband. After that, they held hands and fell asleep to the sound of the ocean sending waves back and forth.

The next day, August stood in the lobby of their resort flipping through pamphlets and checking out the different excursions they could take. They could explore the island, or they could do some extreme water sports, or maybe get a massage on the beach.

Nearby, Samantha was reading a local magazine and saw a feature her husband would want to see.

"August, there is a local tech shop not far from here. You wanna check it out today, sweets?" she asked.

"Actually, yeah, that'd be kinda cool," he said, excited. "If you don't mind, that is. I could scope out the future competition," he added with a wink.

Mouth agape, she replied, "Are you saying that you're considering moving here, sweets? Really?"

August shrugged and said, "Well, yeah, Sam. You love it here, and I know that it's the most relaxed I've ever felt. Why not go for it? We could buy a house right on the beach and live the rest of our lives happy, warm, and sandy."

Samantha threw the magazine on the floor of the lobby and ran to August, leaping into his arms and wrapping her legs around his waist while kissing every square inch of his face.

"OH, SWEETS!" she cried, "I can't believe it! Do you really mean it?"

"I do. I mean, heck," August said, "I fit in here more than in New Dothan. You, on the other hand, still stick out like a sore thumb."

She slapped his arm and then hugged him tight again, replying, "Ok sweets, let's go see this tech shop. Find out if they'll pose any threat to your hostile takeover of Jamaica City's tech scene."

They rolled up to the shop on a rented scooter, Samantha driving and August on the back with his arms wrapped around her. They could've rented two scooters, but August liked holding onto his wife and enjoyed the smell of her dark hair as it blew in the wind surrounding his face. It was an experience he wanted to have as often as possible.

The shop looked no different than most of the other buildings on the island. Bayuss Tech was painted in pastel colors with white accents, preserving the old, relaxed island feel, even though the building was obviously brand new and very modern.

As they entered the store, their happiness turned sour in an instant. Looking around, they had a very odd sense of déjà vu. The very first display they saw was a stand of retro cell-phones made to accept a SmartChip.

"What the hell? They stole my idea," August said, walking over to examine them.

Samantha scanned the rest of the shop while August stared in disbelief at the Bayuss Phone. It was an exact rip-off of his models. They weren't even trying to make it look different. The ports that accept the SmartChip were exactly his design, down to the fingernail groove he put in to make it easier to open.

"Sweets, it gets worse," Samantha said in a worried tone. "You might want to see this."

August rushed over to a table where two lanterns hovered a foot above the surface, changing lights and slowly rotating. A sign on the table told of all the functions that Love.Lanterns possessed. They were, once again, an exact copy of his Life Lanterns. The functions were all exactly the same. Even the lanterns were identical. Instead of using the ones found floating around Jamaica City, these creeps had used the style found in New Dothan.

"What the hell?" August repeated, growing angry. "How... how is this possible?"

Samantha put a hand on his shoulder that almost worked in calming her husband down until August glanced through the window behind the register and saw the workshop in back.

There on the table were pieces of a wooden automaton in a halted state of assembly. It looked a lot like Woodrow, but not the new one. It resembled a full-size version of the original Woodrow, blocky and inorganic like the Montek. Automatons made of metal.

August reached his boiling point. He threw open the door to the back room and rushed in. There were no employees in the shop or the workroom. He began examining their poor attempt at re-creating his wooden automaton. They had everything wrong, and the materials were poor. This thing would never work.

That was a relief, at least.

The sound of a toilet flushing and a door opening caught the couple's attention. Turning to find the source, they were met with a look of astonishment, followed by recognition, and then finally outrage.

"What the hell are you doing in my workshop?" the man hissed as he pushed August in the chest, forcing him back out onto the main sales floor.

"YOU!" August shouted. "You stole my designs. You stole my inventions. How could you do this? And why?"

"Go screw yourself, Mr. Lurie," the tech thief replied. "None of your designs are copyrighted. You foolishly started a company without filing patents for your inventions. All I had to do was buy them and re-create them. I didn't even have to modify the original design because you're a moron."

The customer who had most recently tried to buy the new Woodrow, the man who had bought two phones and two sets of lanterns had a smug look on his face that drove August to clench his fists.

"Joshua Stevens," he said, trying not to punch the man in the face. "You bought my tech just to steal my ideas and sell them as your own. Of course, it's all shitty workmanship, and that wooden hunk of junk in the back will never work. You're a thief and a bastard. But the real question is how did you get the details of the original Woodrow? Montek's legal division confiscated it."

Joshua smiled and pointed to a little sign on the checkout counter, which read:

Bayuss Tech is proudly sponsored by Montek

August couldn't believe what he was seeing. "Are you tellin' me that this ain't really a local small business? It's just an arm of Montek?"

Joshua Stevens folded his arms over his chest, looked down his nose at August, and said, "Maybe that talk at the home office about how smart you are isn't all made up. Yes, we have thousands of small businesses around the world. With everyone's new fascination with trendy, retro tech, Montek couldn't pass up an opportunity to control that market, too."

Samantha reached her boiling point, and said, "Y'all have got to be fucking kidding me. You control the whole damn planet, own every damn thing there is to own... even the government of the United States of Earth. Couldn't you let my husband have this one thing? What the hell is wrong with y'all?"

"Mrs. Lurie, I'm sure you're too simple to understand this," Joshua said, "but we believe your husband invented and created all of this tech while he was an employee with Montek.Automaton. Since I'm now the best they have, they gave me the job of figuring out how all of it works and making versions for Montek... and their many small businesses all over the globe to sell. What you see here is just the beginning."

August was well past angry. Hope was pouring out of his body, and being quickly replaced with the desire just to give up. He couldn't compete with Montek, and would never be able to. They were too big and too powerful.

"Why here, Mr. Stevens?" August asked. "Jamaica City is not exactly known for having a big tech scene."

Joshua walked around and straightened an end cap display, much like he had seen Woodrow do at Sweets, Inc., and replied, "It's close enough yet far enough away. I can drop into your shop and be back here in no time. But management also figured you would never come here. They were apparently wrong about that. We were hoping you'd never see this shop or any like it. We don't want you to be unhappy. Montek would never have opened a store in your little town. Think about it: why should we pay you for what we can just take?"

Samantha started to lead her husband towards the front door. She decided it was time to go, to get the hell out of this shop and Jamaica City.

"Sweets, it's been terrible to meet you. Drop dead, you hear?" she said, opening the front door to Bayuss Tech.

Joshua Stevens, Lead Developer of New Tech for Montek, wasn't done with them just yet.

"I do apologize for all of this, Mr. Lurie," he said coldly. "It is just business. But before you go, I have a proposition for you. You see, the thing my bosses want more than," he gestured around at August's ideas that he had stolen, "all of this inane tech here, is your automaton. Montek wants it. We need it, and we'll pay anything for it."

August stopped moving towards the exit and turned slowly to face this thieving bastard.

"I told you before, Mr. Stevens," he said to Joshua in a dark tone. "Woodrow is like a part of our family. Sam and I made him together. It was… a difficult time in our lives. Buildin' that automaton helped us heal. It made us whole again. So there is no way in hell that I would ever sell him," August said, then raised his voice and yelled, "Much less to fuckin' Montek with their dirty, disgustin' hearts!"

Samantha, in a very unladylike moment, gave Joshua Stevens the finger.

"I understand," Mr. Stevens said, "but we'll be in contact after you've had time to think about it. We're willing to offer you enough Credit so that you never have to work again. You two could travel the entire world for the rest of your lives, staying at the most luxurious resorts. You would live the life of the truly wealthy. All you have to do is sell us Woodrow."

August and Samantha left Bayuss Tech without a word. They packed their suitcases and left Jamaica City a few days early.

CHAPTER 17
NOT A CHANCE

"Patient Lurie, Dr. Granger will see you now."

The same two awful nurses were on duty at the front desk. As soon as they said to go in, the two idiots began laughing and placing bets on something inaudible.

The clinic still looked the same; it had only been a month since the last visit, but it felt less ominous and dark this time. Patient Lurie was happy. Today was a follow-up exam to determine if the prescriptions Dr. Granger had prescribed were completely successful.

While sitting in the exam room waiting for the doctor, there wasn't much to do. Some magazines lay on a side table, so Patient Lurie picked one up and thumbed through it. In the middle of the periodical, there was an advertisement for Montek.Home's newest product — Love.Lanterns.

*FILL YOUR HOME WITH THE LIGHT OF LOVE.
MONTEK.HOME INTRODUCES THE LOVE.LAN-
TERNS; THE PERFECT ADDITION TO ANY HOME.
LET OUR LIGHTS GUIDE YOUR LOVE.*

Patient Lurie threw the magazine into the trash bin while muttering profanities, just as Dr. Granger strode confidently into the room and sat down on a little stool.

"I see here that you're no longer experiencing headaches, trouble with your bowels, or panic attacks," he said in his typical monotone. "That's promising. Today, we'd like to do some more blood work and scans, just to verify that everything is fine. Would you like to add anything before we start? Any new symptoms or changes to tell me about?"

Patient Lurie smiled and replied that there was nothing new or different. It was a good feeling to be free of illness, no matter what Montek was trying to do them. August and Samantha would come out on top as always.

"Ok, good," the doctor said, not sounding like he cared one way or the other. "Follow the nurse and he'll tell you what to do. I'll check in a bit later."

Once all of the blood tests and scans were done, Patient Lurie once again sat in the exam room waiting for the doctor. Once he finally arrived, Dr. Granger didn't even sit down.

He just poked his head in and said, "We're pretty backed up right now, and your tests aren't urgent. You can go home, and we'll call you with the results in a few days if that's ok with you. You'll have to sign a consent form giving us permission to tell you the diagnosis over the Montek.Communication lines. Or, if you'd rather, you can come in for the news. I don't think that will be necessary, though."

Feeling good, Patient Lurie signed the consent form and told the doctor to call, but only on one certain number, as there was no need to worry the spouse.

Despite all that was happening with Montek, the Lurie family was feeling good. Yes, they were stealing August's designs. Yes, they were trying to buy Woodrow. And yes, they were probably going to continue to do both of those things. But August and Samantha were determined not to let it affect them.

Funnily enough, business was still great. In fact, with Montek offering similar tech on the Net, many customers rushed to buy it from Sweets, Inc. to have it faster, and to brag that their model was cooler because it was from a smaller production line. There were fewer Sweets, Inc. versions in the world than the Montek models, which made them rare and better in the eyes of the hip and fashion-conscious citizens of the United States of Earth.

-

August was tinkering with a new invention in the workshop at home when a thought suddenly sprung to his mind.

"Sam, come in here, babe," he called out from his little room full of spare parts and odds and ends he'd packed away. "I've got an idea, and I wanna run it by you."

Sam was hand-washing the dishes from supper, as she liked to do. She said it calmed her down like meditation, even though August had built her an old-style dishwasher. They both hated the SaniDish that Montek sold, which cleaned your kitchenware with ultraviolet light and high-temperature heat. It was waterless, which was technically good for the planet, but both Samantha and August felt that nothing ever got spotless without some water involved.

"Be right there, sweets. Just let me dry my hands," she called back.

As she walked into the workshop, Samantha noticed August was acting a little strange. He was sitting between the lanterns, which were shining a dim and somewhat melancholy light in the small room. August seemed nervous and was tapping his foot while chewing on his fingernails. When he looked up and saw Samantha, he smiled and held out his arms for a hug.

"I think I forgot to tell you, but dinner was amazin', honey. Just amazin'," he said as he squeezed her tight.

Samantha loved it when August complimented her cooking. She didn't cook as much as before when she had the restaurant, but she tried to cook at least once a day. It was still her passion, but cooking also brought up a lot of bad memories.

"You did forget to say so, but I forgive you, you handsome devil," she replied, thumping the end of his nose.

August kissed Sam on the neck, and she squirmed a little. It tickled, but it also felt extraordinarily pleasant.

"So, I wanted to talk to you about Montek's offer," he said, getting serious.

Samantha pushed away from him with a shocked look and said, "Sweets, you aren't honestly considering selling Woodrow to Montek, are you?"

August scrunched up his face in disgust and said, "Hell no! Not a chance, babe. Not a chance. No, I was thinkin' of sellin' them the SameSoul. You said you didn't like it, and I know they'd pay us an incredible amount of Credit for it. We could travel. We could go and do it... live like nomads. Never stayin' in one place for too long. Get out there and experience the world, you know? It's all I've ever wanted to do, and I think this could be our ticket. What do you say?"

Samantha wasn't sure what to think. On the one hand, she honestly didn't like the thought of her soul... or consciousness... or whatever... being captured inside some machine, even if it was lovely old Woodrow. On the other hand, she would love to leave all of this behind and be happy with her husband; no worries about what Montek might or might not steal next. Just travel the world and be happy. Learn recipes from around the globe. It sounded like pure Heaven to her the more Sam thought about it.

"Oh, sweets," she said, sounding unsure. "It sounds wonderful... except that you'd be helping that disgusting bunch of maggots at Montek. And to be honest, I was kind of coming around to the idea of the SameSoul."

She wasn't coming around, not completely anyways. But it wouldn't hurt to let August think she was. After all, he was very proud of his invention, as he should be. Samantha kept thinking back to how they would have done it to Tara if she had activated that damned BrainSave. If it was good enough for her, it was good enough for Sam. But she also thought of being trapped forever in a tin can...or, in this case, a woodblock, and it terrified Samantha.

"Well, babe," August said with a surprised grin on his face, "I could always keep the original for us and sell Montek a copy... or heck, just sell them the plans to make the SameSoul. We could even take Woodrow with us. I don't know, I just feel like we're stuck in a bad situation with these jerks, so we might as well try to make the best of it."

Woodrow had been folding laundry in the other room when he had heard his name, and suddenly pushed the workshop door open and wedged inside with the two of them.

"WOOD ROW," it said.

Both Samantha and August snickered at the big, wooden robot. He always came whenever he heard his name, just like a dog.

"No, Woody, we don't need you right now, sweets," Samantha told it. "Go on back to folding the laundry, please and thank you."

Woodrow did as he was instructed, leaving the two humans alone again.

"So, what do you think, sweetheart?" August asked. "Sell this little device, make a ton of Credit, and travel the world? Live like royalty in a different country every month?"

Taking a brief moment to consider, Samantha's teeth broke free in an explosive moment of happiness as she screamed, "Yes, baby, yes! Please and thank you, too! Let's do it. Let's do it now!"

August was thrilled. He thought it was the absolute best move for them. After all of the awful things they had endured together, he felt they deserved to celebrate their life by doing this. It just felt right.

Samantha was in shock. She never for one minute thought that her life would have turned out like this. It felt like she deserved to have a wonderful life after all of the difficulties that had come their way in the past. Together, they had been through quite a lot, and it felt like the right time to celebrate that life by making this crazy move.

"It's settled, then," August said, slapping his knees and standing up. "I'll call up Joshua Stevens tomorrow and offer to sell him the SameSoul. Of course, I'll have to tell him about it first. Montek don't know anythin' about it, but I guarantee they'll want it once they know about it."

"Oh, sweets I'm so happy I could spit!" Sam said. "This is the best idea you've ever had. I'm going to the bedroom to start weeding through my old clothes and throwing out everything I don't need anymore. Our lives are going to have to fit into suitcases now!"

August planted a kiss on Samantha's forehead before she walked back out of the workshop and told her, "I'll be out in a bit to do the same, babe. I just wanna finish this little hunk of junk I'm workin' on."

Five minutes later one of their cellphones rang.

"Hello?"

"Patient Lurie? This is Dr. Granger. I'm calling in regard to your follow-up blood work and scans. You signed a form that gave me consent to contact you by phone, so I decided to go ahead and do this over the phone rather than set up an appointment."

Patient Lurie was dead silent, hoping for good news but fearing the worst, as that's what life had taught them to expect recently.

"Well, the good news is that the cure worked, and your stomach cancer is completely gone," the doctor explained, "with all of the internal damage having been fully healed by the second set of meds I prescribed."

Patient Lurie exhaled a sigh of utter and total relief. It had worked. Everything was better, and there was nothing to fear anymore. Thank God.

"There is some bad news, I'm afraid," Dr. Granger added, not sounding as if the news was awful. "You see, Patient Lurie, after this was cleared up and we checked your blood work and scans again, we noticed a different anomaly. Tracing it back through your proteins, we found something else."

"What?" Patient Lurie asked with a dry rasp.

There was a long pause on the line, and Patient Lurie could only wait in dreaded silence for the answer that felt certain to be only one thing.

But no, it couldn't be that bad. Things were going so well for the Lurie family. It couldn't be that. Not a chance.

"Patient Lurie," the doctor said over the line, "your Countdown has begun. You have five days."

CHAPTER 18
DAY ONE

The decision whether or not to tell your spouse that you are going to die in the next five days seems like an easy one. You can't just keep it secret from them. That would be terrible, wouldn't it?

Or would it be kinder to keep them in the dark? Would you rather spend your last five days crying and feeling sorry for yourself, or would you rather spend them planning for a trip around the world? That way, your spouse could still go on the journey without you to get away from all of the bad memories in this house.

It seemed like the better option, and so that is exactly what Patient Lurie decided to do. Keep it secret, and go ahead with the planning. It would not be easy either way at the end of the five days, but it seemed like this way, at least, their last five days together would be pleasant.

—

"Mr. Stevens?" August said.

There was a momentary pause on the other end, and a deep inhalation of breath before Joshua said, "Mr. Lurie! I can't believe you're calling! Have you changed your mind about your automaton? I promise you that you won't regret it. You'll be rich beyond your wildest dreams."

Once again, August wondered if he was making the right decision to sell his invention to this global network of crooks and monsters. He had sounded so confident when talking to Samantha about this in his workshop, but that was more to put her mind at ease. Inside, he still felt guilty about the thought of taking Credit and living like a king while Montek took his hard work and put their dirty signature all over it.

"No, Mr. Stevens," August said, trying to hide his disgust. "I will not be sellin' you Woodrow. I've told you that won't happen."

Joshua Stevens's voice went from happy to irritated in an instant, as he heaved an enormous sigh and grunted in reply, "Then why have you tied up my line and wasted my time, Mr. Lurie? I have a business to run."

"You mean stealin' other people's ideas and passin' them off as Montek's original inventions?" August let slip, immediately regretting the words, as he was trying to get Mr. Stevens on his side temporarily.

"Mr. Lurie, go fu…"

Before Mr. Stevens could finish that thought, August interrupted and said, "I'm sorry that was rude of me, Mr. Stevens. I do have somethin' to discuss with you. Somethin' that I think you'll be very interested in. I know it's somethin' that Montek would love to get a hold of."

Joshua's attitude changed to positive once more as he replied, "Well, now. I am interested. I'll be at your shop tonight. Will 7 pm work for you?"

"Mr. Stevens," August said, sounding confused, "don't you even want to hear about it? You have no clue what it is I am tryin' to sell you."

"Look, August," Mr. Stevens said, "I won't bullshit you. If it's something you came up with, then I am going to want it. And if I want it, Montek wants it. I'll see you at 7:00."

Joshua disconnected the call without another word.

Samantha snuck up behind her husband who was standing in between the lanterns just staring at his cellphone in a confused silence. She had overheard a little of his side of the conversation and knew that he had been talking to that thief Joshua Stevens. It bothered her that they had to deal with him. It bothered her that they were going to deal with Montek at all. But it was for the best. The Credit Montek would pay for the SameSoul would cover any expense the Lurie family ever had for the rest of their lives.

She put her arms around August's waist and whispered in his ear, "Sweets, I was just getting rid of some old clothes, and I found some pretty sexy underwear. I need your help to decide whether to keep it or not."

August had not heard his wife walk in and jumped at her touch. Once he recovered and turned around, he had to do a double take… giving Samantha a once-over from top to bottom, taking in every inch of her body. To his surprise, she was not wearing any sexy underwear for him to look at.

"Uh… what sexy underwear, babe?" he asked, his mouth going dry and his pulse quickening. "You're nekkid as a jay bird."

"Oops. Whatever shall we do now?" she pushing her body against August.

Her husband ran his calloused hands up and down her silky smooth skin. The juxtaposition of his rough, dark complexion against her soft, tanned skin always made him smile. He smelled her long, black hair, and the aroma combined with the touch of her naked body made him instantly hard. In between the lanterns, he looked at his wife and smiled.

"I have a few ideas," he told her, "but you're gonna have to sign a waiver."

Samantha pushed back from him with a crooked grin on her face, and feigning shock, said, "A waiver, sweets? Whatever for?"

August spun her around and pushed her towards the dinner table in a rush, and answered, "I can't be held responsible for how quickly this will be over. You're butt nekkid and sexier than anyone has any right to be. I just don't want you gettin' all angry at me for finishin' before you do."

Samantha put her hand under his shirt and ran her fingernails up and down his back. August groaned and pulled her tighter to him.

She grabbed his face in both of her hands, and in a stern voice said, "I'll sign yours, as long as you sign mine, which states you must use any means necessary to make amends, sweets."

At that, August picked her up, placed her on the table, and stripped naked as fast as he could. Samantha put her feet on top of the table, making it easy for him. She bit at his lip as he worked. August braced himself on the table's edge with his hands, pushed with his feet for strength, using his hips for the intricate movements. Back and forth. Over and over.

After a while, Samantha realized that her husband had lied to her, as she finished long before he did. August was untiring, more so than he had been in a long time. More so than her husband had ever been, if truth be told.

Samantha came again and shrieked in triumph. She grabbed onto her husband and urged him to go faster and harder, wanting him to feel that same moment of pure joy. He finally did, and then fell onto his wife. Sam held him, both of them gasping for air and smiling as they tried to move, but couldn't. Eventually, August pushed himself up just enough to kiss the love of his life. She held onto his face while they shared each other's oxygen. It lasted for as long as either could stand before they broke apart. The lanterns hovered in the air, slowly changing from warm to cool colors. They rotated around the table, creating a calming effect.

August had tears in his eyes as they pulled apart. Samantha did, too.

"Sweets, why are you crying?" she whispered.

August wiped at his tears, feeling a little embarrassed and said, "Me? Why are you cryin'?"

Samantha smiled and rubbed her hand down his chest, wiping at the sweat dripping down his torso.

"Because I love you so damn much that it hurts," she told him. "And I just came twice… That don't happen to a shy Southern lady like myself every day, you know?"

August wiped at the sweat running down the back of his head and looked away.

"Shy, my ass," he replied. "But I love you so much it hurts, too, babe." He paused, fighting back more tears before going on. "I was also thinkin' that I'm gonna miss this place. That was one of the last times we're ever gonna have sex in this house."

Samantha laughed. "Sweets, if you promise it'll be like that every time, we can fuck five times a day before we leave."

August's eyes went wide with shock, and he gasped, "Such language from a shy country girl! And I can't make any promises about it always bein' that great. I'm only a man, not a machine."

"Well, maybe I'll talk to Woodrow about it, then, sweets," she said in a husky voice and winked at her man slyly.

His eyes shot open even further as he said, "You ain't gonna be gettin' freaky with Woodrow, woman. I won't have you defilin' our robot."

At that moment, having heard his name called twice, Woodrow marched into the kitchen and found them both naked and lying together on the table.

"WOOD ROW CLEAN?" it said.

They both burst into laughter while Woodrow waited patiently for an answer.

"No, Woodrow, sweets," Samantha replied in between guffaws. "You don't have to clean. Go back into the living room and enter power down mode, please and thank you."

Woodrow trundled out of the room, making a noise like a baby playing with wooden blocks. Samantha watched him go and remembered why August had made her original small, wooden sculpture into an automaton. It was because she so despised the big metallic and soulless Montek. Automatons that were becoming popular at the time. Now they were just about everywhere, and functioning on tech that her husband had designed. Strange how time messes with your life like that.

Montek had, for lack of a better word, stolen the original Woodrow. Then later, she and August built a larger, full-size wooden automaton. The new Woodrow was a vital part of their lives. He assisted August run the shop, cleaned the whole house, did lots of chores, helped do the shopping, and was even learning to be a sous-chef of sorts, and... well, was just always around. She couldn't imagine their lives without Woodrow.

In a way, he was just wood and string. He walked and talked, but didn't mean anything. On the other hand, he was more advanced in many ways than the current Montek.Automaton models, which was why Montek wanted to get their hands on him so badly. The upper management at Montek must have realized they burnt a crucial bridge when they fired August over the factory accident. Now Montek needed to reverse-engineer this odd, wooden robot to make improvements on their line of automatons, because improvements often meant new models, and new models always meant more Credit. But the Luries would never sell Woodrow, no matter what happened to them, she thought.

August watched Woodrow leave and felt a tinge of sadness because he loved that clunky, wooden oddity. He had built the original Woodrow out of a wooden sculpture his wife had made for him, but once Montek stole it, he and Samantha had created this new one together. Woodrow was vital to their everyday lives, and a symbol of their feelings about Montek and the modern world. He would never sell Woodrow to Montek. Even though what was coming would change everything. It didn't matter. They'd never have him.

"Woodrow should go on the journey, too. He's earned it, sweets," Samantha blurted out.

August had just come to the same realization as his wife. It wouldn't be that hard to arrange the transport of an automaton for human companionship. People did it all the time with Montek.Automatons. Why not with Woodrow? It was a great idea. August had made his mind up. Tickets would be booked for Woodrow as well.

"Absolutely, Sam," he said. "He does deserve to come along. He can help carry all your bags."

August winked at Samantha this time. As they were still naked and on the table, she didn't have many ways to retaliate, so she lightly slapped his butt.

"No, he can carry your bags, sweets," she replied.

August looked away, in the direction that Woodrow had gone, shrugged his shoulders, and replied, "He'll be a big help."

CHAPTER 19
BELIEVE IT

Joshua Stevens arrived precisely at 7 pm, pulling up to Sweets, Inc. in Montek.Drive's newest model AutoCar. It was worth more Credit than some of the houses back on August's street. Mr. Stevens strode into the shop with a shit-eating grin on his clean-shaven face.

"Ok, Mr. Lurie," he said, rubbing his hands greedily. "Show me what you want us to buy. I have a feeling it's a game-changer. Am I right?"

August could sense that Mr. Stevens was nervous. He was full of restless energy. Maybe it wasn't nerves, though. Maybe it was just excitement. Either way, it made August uncomfortable.

"Why do you think it's gonna be any good at all?" August asked. "How do you know I ain't just yankin' your chain, Mr. Stevens?"

Joshua spread his arms and stretched his smile even further across his chiseled features.

"Because you're a nice guy, August," he answered. "And a fricking genius. I'm betting that whatever it is you got tucked away is worth a fortune to the both of us. So let's not waste any more time. Show me the goods."

August once again questioned if this was a good idea, but it was too late. The plans were in motion, and he needed this Credit to see them through. Samantha deserved a new life with relaxation and luxury at every destination.

"Alright, Mr. Stevens," August said, "do you remember the invention of the BrainSave, and how it was a marvel of modern tech? And do you remember all of the upgrades I made to that chip when I worked for Montek.Automaton?"

Joshua nodded along to the rhetorical questions, as they were just about to set up the big reveal. He was getting very anxious about finding out what August had created.

"Well, the one limitation that I could never seem to get past," August continued, "just kept hauntin' me. Even after Montek screwed me over. Do you know what it was?"

Joshua shook his head. He had no clue what the brilliant inventor was trying to say. After all of the work August had done on the BrainSave, it was already a work of art in its present state. It was a piece of tech that blew everything else out of the water.

"I have no idea, Mr. Lurie," he answered, his breathing coming more rapidly.

"The limitation was," August explained, "it was just tech. It was only a machine. It was just a dang old robot."

Joshua's heart dropped.

He looked confused and said, "Mr. Lurie, it is just a robot. That's the whole idea; to make people feel like their loved ones are still with them. Put some memories in the tin can, and simulate the experience of talking with those who have passed on. That's all it is, and all it ever can be."

August pulled out the SameSoul and placed it on the counter. It was visually very similar to the BrainSave. It had to be to make the transition from the BrainSave to the SameSoul easier. If they had to retrofit every unsold Montek.Automaton in storage it wouldn't be as financially beneficial to Montek.

Once Joshua Stevens picked it up and examined the chip, he was shocked by the complexity of what he found there.

"That's not true anymore, Mr. Stevens," August stated flatly. "This is the SameSoul. It takes everythin' you are, your full consciousness, and puts it into an automaton. You will continue to live from inside a machine. Your same thoughts, your same memories, your same fears... absolutely everythin'. You will be you."

Joshua's jaw fell open. He looked at the little package in his hand and placed it back on the counter.

"So, it can make new memories?" he asked. "Simulate emotion? Is it artificial intelligence you've created?"

August just shook his head. He didn't get it yet.

"No, Mr. Stevens, nothin' like that. It ain't a simulation of life. It ain't a program," August said, trying to simplify it for the man. "It's a vessel for the human consciousness. It's never-endin' life."

Mr. Stevens looked down at the floor and rubbed his chin. He paced back and forth for a few breaths, then snapped his head up and locked eyes with August.

"I'll be right back," he said in an emotionless tone. "Wait here, Mr. Lurie."

Joshua Stevens spun on his heels and marched right out of the store. He got into his AutoCar and began rapidly talking to himself. August could only sit and stare, as he had no idea what was going on. Was Mr. Stevens impressed? Did he want to buy it? August sure hoped so; otherwise all these plans would come to a crashing halt.

After a few minutes, Mr. Stevens came back into the store with a serious look on his face.

He strode right up to August, pointed at his cellphone, and said, "You're going to receive a call in just a minute, August. It will be from the head of Montek.Automaton, Chadwick Sheppard."

August felt numb for a second. One of the richest men in the entire world was going to call his cellphone?

"Why is he gonna call me?" August asked. "I ain't got nothin' to say to him. If y'all want my tech, I'll sell it. But it's gonna cost you a lot of Credit, you hear?"

Joshua placed his hands on his hips, looked the brilliant inventor right in the eyes, and told him, "He wants to talk to you in person because I told him I don't believe you. I don't think your tech can do what you say it does."

August almost called the whole thing off right then.

"Believe it, jack," he snapped, snatching the SameSoul from the counter. "This ain't no joke. If I say it can, then it can. I don't lie."

"You can tell it to…"

August's cellphone began to ring.

He picked it up and answered the call. "Hello, this is August Lurie. How may I help you?"

"Mr. Lurie," a voice said on the other end, "it's fantastic to speak with you at last. My name is Chadwick Sheppard. I'm very sorry about the negative experiences you've had with us in the past. Your wrongful termination, the theft of your ideas and inventions, the bad attitude from Mr. Stevens, and anything else that has put a bad taste in your mouth. I intend to right all of those wrongs today."

August honestly didn't know what to say. He was flabbergasted. An employee of Montek was apologizing for all of the horrible shit they had put him and Samantha through.

And not just any employee: it was Chadwick Sheppard. The head of Montek.Automaton. The third-richest man in the world.

"Well, Mr. Sheppard…"

"Please, August. Call me Chad."

"Ok, Chad," August said, "I appreciate your kind words and all, but you'll excuse me if I don't entirely trust everythin' you're sayin' to me. Y'all have done me pretty wrong, and I've come to terms with that. All I want is to sell you this tech so that my wife and I can retire right now, today, and travel the world. No more working, no more stress. You offer me enough Credit and the SameSoul is yours."

"All in good time, August. All in good time," the immensely wealthy son of a bitch said. "First, let me ask you a few questions. You see, Mr. Stevens doesn't believe your tech is what you say it is. Can you tell me why he should? How do you know it will perform the way you say it will? Have you tested it?"

"Well, no," August answered honestly. "It's all theoretical at this point; that's true. I ain't tested it, but I know it will work. Everythin' I make works the way it should. Believe it. Or, hell, don't. If you don't want to buy it, I'll just market it myself and Montek can kiss my ass."

Chadwick Sheppard laughed over the line, seeming to enjoy August's angry response.

"I do believe you, August," Chadwick said. "I've seen the upgrades you made while working for us. I've seen the tech you made after you left. I have full confidence that if you say it will work… it will work. I just wanted to see if you believed it. And it seems that you do. I'd like to make you an offer now."

Mr. Stevens smiled satisfactorily as he drove away. August was smiling, too. He was sure that Chadwick Sheppard was probably laughing far away in his opulent office.

At least they were all happy.

Mr. Sheppard had offered August the most unbelievable sum of Credit imaginable. All he had to do was give the blue-prints to Joshua right then and sign over all of the rights to the SameSoul. They let him have the only working model as a keepsake.

And now Samantha and August had more Credit than any-one else in Alabama. They had more Credit than most peo-ple on planet Earth. There would be no more hard work or stress. It was all over. His beautiful wife would get the kind of life she deserved.

August gathered all of his personal effects from around the store and put them into a box. He grabbed a sign for his Life Lanterns and scribbled a message on the back. He walked out of Sweets, Inc. and left the door wide open, placing the sign on the window sill as he walked away from the shop he and his wife had worked so hard to start. The culmination of their hard work and all of the merchandise still in stock didn't matter anymore. He walked away from it all. The sign that he left behind said:

CLOSING SALE. ALL ITEMS ARE NOW FREE OF CHARGE. TAKE ONLY WHAT YOU NEED AND LEAVE THE REST FOR SOMEONE ELSE. THANKS FOR YOUR SUPPORT.

Samantha paced the house. She was a nervous wreck. August hadn't called and let her know how things were going. Did he sell the SameSoul? Would they get enough Credit for what was to come? August needed this. He had worked so hard with Sweets, Inc., and with Montek before that. He had earned an early retirement. So what if they were only in their thirties? If Montek was going to pay significant Credit, then retirement it would be.

Just as she was mulling over how useful Woodrow would be on this lifelong trip around the world, helping August so he could still invent and work with tech the way he liked to do, the front door was thrown open and scared Samantha half to death.

"Honey, I'm home!" August called out loudly.

Samantha ran to him and slapped his arm a little bit harder than if she were only kidding.

"You scared the heck out of me, sweets!" she exclaimed. "Why didn't you call? What's the word? Did they buy the SameSoul? Are we free?"

August looked down at his feet and stuck his hands into his pockets. He kicked at invisible piles of dirt, as if embarrassed.

"Well, I wanted to surprise you is why I didn't call," August said ashamedly. "Mr. Stevens came by the shop, and I told him about the SameSoul, but he didn't believe me."

"He didn't believe you?" Sam asked incredulously. "Why on Earth not?"

"Well, I only have the one untested prototype, you see. Can you blame him for not takin' me at my word?"

Samantha shook her head. She had never even considered that it wouldn't work. Everything August made always worked. Why wouldn't the people at Montek know that?

"So they didn't want it?" she said, her voice growing tight with worry. "What are we going to do, sweets?"

August patted the air with his hands to calm Samantha down. "Now hold on, babe. I didn't say that," he said. "Mr. Stevens called the home office, and someone else wanted to talk to me. This new fella believed me and made me an offer."

Samantha felt relieved instantly. The Credit wasn't the important thing, not even close. As long as the journey could still happen... as long as August would get to travel the world like he had always dreamed... that is what mattered. "So you dealt with a real management type, huh?" she said, acting impressed. "Fancy that, sweets!"

August finally looked up to make eye contact, a mischievous look on his face as she said, "It was Chadwick Sheppard, babe."

Samantha almost fell onto the couch.

"Chadwick Sheppard?" she gasped. "One of the richest men in the world? The head of Montek.Automaton?"

"The one and only, babe," August replied, dusting invisible dirt from his shoulders. "He believed me... and he offered me a lot of Credit for my tech, babe. A lot of Credit. More than we will ever use. We are rich, Sam. Super-rich. Like... here, just take a look at our account."

Samantha took the cellphone from his extended hand and looked at the screen, which showed their account summary. The number of zeros on the display had to be some kind of error. There was no way that they had that much Credit in the bank.

She gazed up with a bewildered look that then spread into a huge grin. August felt a wave of warmth spread through his chest. Samantha would get to take the journey around the world that she deserved. After all of the horrible things she has had to deal with over the years, he was content with the knowledge that she would never have to worry about any-thing ever again.

"I can't believe it, sweets."

"Believe it, Sam."

"I guess we better get packing, then," she said. "What are you going to do about the shop?"

August took his phone back and stuck it into his pocket, then shrugged his shoulders.

"I gave it all away," he told her. "Just left the door open and put up a sign that asked people only to take one thing each."

Samantha threw her head back and laughed.

"You know that the first person who comes by is going to take the sign down and call his friends to come empty the shop out so that they can sell it all themselves, right? Tell me you know that, sweets."

August just shrugged his shoulders again, and said, "It don't matter, babe. None of it matters anymore. We're gonna be fine."

Samantha reached over and held his hands in her own.

"Yes, we will be," she answered.

Of course, only one of them knew that was a lie.

CHAPTER 28
DAY TWO

August woke up angry. At first, he couldn't pinpoint why he was so furious, but after thinking it about for a moment, he knew exactly why. Samantha lay beside him, still asleep and snoring softly. Oblivious to her husband's internal struggles, she smiled in her sleep. It should have made him feel better; it usually did. But even his wife's beautiful face couldn't work its usual magic this morning.

He got out of bed and went to use the toilet. In the bathroom, he found Woodrow in powered down mode. August woke the wooden automaton with a brushing touch on its shoulder as he passed.

"Mornin', Woody. How's it hangin', man?"

Woodrow clacked to life with a sound like four baseball bats knocking together.

"MORN NING," it said in reply.

After flushing, August decided to work out some of his aggression in the workshop. Tinkering with tech always calmed him down. The night before, in discussion with Samantha about what would happen next, they had decided to keep the house and not get rid of everything. She had said that it might be nice to have a home-base they could return to every once in a while. He tried to remember her exact words —

"When you need to feel comforted, where do you go? If you ever feel completely out of sorts and lost, the best place to go is always home. This is our home, Auggie, sweets. Let's not abandon it the way you did your shop."

And she had been right. After thinking about it, it would be nice for Samantha to have all the wonderful kitchen appliances he had made for her waiting for her here at the house should she ever feel the need to use them.

Right now, he was glad they hadn't just gotten rid of everything immediately the way he had with Sweets, Inc. Not that he regretted doing it. August didn't need those things anymore, and giving all of it away just felt right. They certainly didn't need the Credit anymore, now that they were extremely wealthy.

Recalling the number of zeros in their account still felt weird. To know they could just up and buy almost anything they wanted right now was an unfamiliar feeling.

Lost in thought, August banged his elbow on the corner of his workbench, the old one that he had built long ago when living in that dump of an apartment on West Main Street. He swore a string of expletives and called out for the lanterns to come into the room and light the place how he liked it while tinkering.

They floated in and hovered above him, creating a warm glow in the room that made no shadows, and lit the little workspace evenly on all sides.

"Now where the hell did I put that SameSoul?" he asked himself.

August looked all over his bench for it. Under all the mess he always somehow seemed to have there, on the floor, in the waste receptacle (maybe Woodrow had tossed it out?), but he couldn't find it.

"Oh well. I probably left it in my other pants," he said sleepily, still groggy from restless sleep. "I'll get it later."

He didn't need it right now, honestly; August just wanted to run some more diagnostics on the small and amazing device. After all of that talk yesterday about whether or not it would work, August just wanted to reassure himself. He was certain he had brought it home from the shop, and he was positive that Joshua Stevens hadn't taken it. Well, almost positive.

–

Samantha woke up feeling happy. Things weren't perfect, they never were and never would be, but today was going to be a great day. Yesterday had been a little stressful, but with the incredible sex in the kitchen, and the amount of Credit August had received for his SameSoul blueprints, things were looking up.

"Always look on the bright side, as they used to say," she muttered to herself as she slid out of bed.

And that is exactly what Samantha was doing today: looking on the bright side. She went to use the bathroom, and afterward, Samantha went in search of her husband. It was silent in the house, so she knew he wasn't watching any vids or shows. And that meant he was probably in the workshop.

On the way, she noticed the SameSoul prototype sitting on the kitchen counter, where August had left it last night. She picked it up to bring it to August in the workshop, but before she could enter there was a loud POP from inside his fortress of tinkering. She rushed to the workshop door, but just as she reached for the handle, August burst out with a fierce look on his face.

"Sweets!" she cried out, startled to hell and back. "What's wrong? What happened?"

August looked at the troubled expression on Samantha's face, and decided not to bother her with his worries, the reasons he was upset, and why he had made such a bonehead mistake in his shop just now.

"I'm sorry, Sam," he said sweetly, kissing her on the forehead. "I hope I didn't scare you or nothin'. I was just messin' around in there, tryin' to come up with somethin' new, but my mind was… elsewhere and I fed too much Tesla energy into a small motor. It… well, it blew up in my dang face."

"Are you hurt? Do we need to go to the clinic, sweets?" she asked.

August shook his head quickly and replied, "No, even if I were hurt I wouldn't want to go back there ever again."

Samantha looked at him curiously, then recalled all the bad memories they shared at that awful place.

"Alright, sweets," she said, returning his kiss with a little peck on August's cheek. "Why don't you go shower, and I'll make us some breakfast. How do cheese grits and bacon sound?"

He suddenly felt a good deal better at the mention of her food. Samantha had been cooking less and less lately, which worried August. She lived to cook and loved to do it. It was sad to see her glance into a kitchen full of her favorite stuff, but not have the desire to cook so much as buttered toast.

"Shoot, babe, that sounds real good," August said, sidling up close to his wife and hugging her tight. "Did I ever tell you that I love you?"

"Yes, as a matter of fact, you might have mentioned it a time or two," she said, returning his embrace and breathing in the smell of his shirt. "I love you, too, man of mine. Now get. I've got some work to do."

Once she heard the shower running, Samantha began to cry. She sobbed deep and long, gasping for breath when she could. There were so many things going through her head at that moment. August was acting differently, and it worried her. The home that they had known for so long, Cheryl's old house, would soon be empty of life. Everything was piling up inside of her to the point where it all came out as tears. Sure, she was sad. She was worried. Samantha was regretting past decisions. But mostly she was just overwhelmed with everything and needed to let it out.

She didn't want to bother August with her worries and problems — not with everything that was going on. He had enough to worry about. Samantha looked down and noticed the SameSoul on the counter again. She picked it up and placed it in her apron pocket so she would remember to give it to him later.

Samantha was still puzzled as to why he had kept this prototype. What was he going to use it for, anyways? She didn't want to be trapped in some little box and not get to join her friends and family in Heaven. And she didn't want her husband, the love of her life, to be trapped inside it, either.

The shower stopped, and Samantha noticed that the food was done. She had been thinking so deeply that she had just cooked on auto.

"Well, damn," she said to herself. "I hope it tastes good. I don't remember seasoning a thing!"

But before she could taste anything, Samantha heard footsteps approaching from behind.

"Sam," August suddenly whispered into her ear, "I'm sure it's as delicious as always. Your food never disappoints."

They sat down and ate breakfast together. Sam felt less sad, and August seemed less mad. Neither one of them wanted to bother their spouse with negative talk, so August and Samantha only discussed positive subjects.

"I told you, babe!" he said, excited. "These are probably the best grits I have ever had! You've outdone yourself this time."

Samantha grinned as her husband ate slowly, savoring every bite; exactly how you should eat real food. She spooned some grits into her mouth and thought August must be just being nice. The grits were ok, but it for sure wasn't her best. They were almost bland.

After they cleaned up together, August grabbed his bike helmet and headed for the front door. He didn't say a word; he seemed lost in his own thoughts.

"Sweets, where are you going?" Samantha asked him.

Surprised at being interrupted, he spun around suddenly to see Sam standing in the kitchen looking at him curiously.

"Oh! Uh, sorry, Sam," he said haltingly. "I'm… gonna to ride up to the shop and… see how it looks. I'm just wonderin' if you were right and if it's already empty."

"Well, hold on a minute and I'll come with you, sweets," she said, wanting to spend some time with him. "Just let me get my helmet, too."

August held up his hand to stop her.

"Babe, I kinda just want to go alone," he said, not making eye contact with his wife. "I'm sorry, babe. I just got a lot on my mind and wanna ride a little bit before checkin' on the shop. Is that alright with you?"

Sam felt relieved. She wasn't feeling much like going anywhere at the moment, although she didn't want to be apart from August either.

"Ok, sweets," she told him. "But please don't be gone long. I need you here with me, ok?"

August smiled wide and walked over to embrace her. He held her tight to his chest and breathed in deeply her long, beautiful hair, a smell that always made him feel like everything was going to be ok.

"You got it, love," he murmured. "I'll be back real soon."

Once he left, Sam wiped her hands on the apron before

taking it off. Doing so, she felt the SameSoul in her pocket and realized she had forgotten once again to give it to August. Right away, she took it out and placed it on the dinner table where he was sure to see it when he came home.

-

August hated lying. He was all about telling the truth as much as possible. But when it came to Samantha, he loved her so much that he would do anything to spare her feelings. August didn't want to upset her one little bit. The entire bike ride to the shop he felt guilty about lying to his wife, even though it was only to keep her from being worried or hurt. His only consolation was that it would all be ok soon. Just a few more days and she would never have to worry again. No stress, no problems. Credit couldn't solve everything, but it could make your life easier and more relaxing.

He pulled to a screeching halt in front of the shop and noticed right away that his sign was gone. Samantha was usually right about everything, and it seemed like this time was no exception.

August glanced inside through the shop window and found that it was empty. No merchandise on the shelves at all. But he didn't care about that. He was here for one reason only: to find the SameSoul. He was sure the last time he had it was here, as he sold the blueprints and copyrights of it to Joshua

Stevens. He had never meant to give them the prototype, and Chadwick Sheppard had even insisted that August keep it. So where was it? Had Mr. Stevens stolen the SameSoul? It was driving August crazy because he needed that little box. He had plans for it.

CHAPTER 21
LOST AND FOUND

Samantha was lying in bed when August got home. She heard the door slam shut and quickly got up to see him. He was still visibly upset when she came upon him drinking some water in the kitchen.

"Sweets, what is going on? Why are you so upset? Please talk to me," Sam pleaded.

August finished gulping down the water and looked down at his feet. Despite the desire to keep her from being hurt or upset, he was going to have to tell her what was going on. Well, some of it at least.

"It's a bunch of stuff really," he said, starting off slowly. "I mean… I know that we're like wealthy now and I should be focusin' on different cultures, and lyin' on beaches sippin' on exotic drinks and all that. But I'm scared. What if somethin' happens to me? Will you be ok out there on your own? Probably, but…"

212

Samantha started to protest, but August just held up his hands, wanting to get it all out as quickly as possible, and said, "Hang on, let me finish."

She rolled her eyes and motioned for him to keep going.

"So, the idea of Woodrow goin' on this trip started me thinkin' about stuff," he continued. "We have the SameSoul, right? I could bring it and use it if somethin' were to happen to me. That way, I could always be there for you, Sam. You wouldn't have to be alone. I could still do this trip with you. Wouldn't you like that?"

Samantha bit her lip, quite harder than she meant to do, and gasped a bit as she tasted the coppery blood hit her tongue.

"Yes, sweets," she admitted. "I think that using Woodrow as a vessel to contain one of us has always been part of the plan, whether we knew it or not. The SameSoul does take it a step further, and make it so if something bad happened, we could still be together for longer. But what about that has got you so upset?"

Samantha didn't want to make things worse by telling him her continued reservations about using his tech, and her fear that it would keep one of their souls from entering Heaven.

"I can't find it, babe," August said, his voice trembling. "It's lost. Or maybe Mr. Stevens stole it. I can't remember ever bringin' it home. The last time I remember havin' it in my hands was at the shop. And you were right. The shop was totally ransacked. They took everything. Even the sign I made was missin'. There's nothin' there anymore. It's just gone... my greatest invention ever is lost."

August sat at the table and put his head down. Samantha felt terrible about what she was going to do next, but in her opinion, it had to be done. Things had changed, and so she had also changed her mind. Sam reached over and picked up the SameSoul, which was sitting across the table from August, who had not even noticed it in his agitated state of mind.

Samantha dropped it into her purse, which also sat on the table top.

"Sweets, I'm so sorry," she said, admitting to more than he knew. "I know that it meant a lot to you, but look on the bright side, as they used to say. You can always make another one. You designed it. You have all the same materials in your workshop, don't you?"

August looked up and morosely nodded. "Yeah, but the thing is, babe, I signed a contract statin' that I wouldn't make any more of them," he said solemnly. "I gave my word, and I'm legally bound not to build another SameSoul ever again. It's Montek's property now. That's what burns. I sold it to pay for the rest of our lives, Sam. But I'm startin' to regret it."

Samantha felt awful, but couldn't let him know that she had it. Not now. She had made her mind up about that. August would not be putting himself into that SameSoul.

"Listen, sweets. You can buy one of theirs once they start making them," she offered, knowing that it was the wrong thing to say.

August looked up at her with a disgusted expression and said, "Do you really think that I'd do that, babe?"

"Not in a million years, sweets," she admitted. "But I figured I'd offer it up as a suggestion anyway. Can't hurt, can it?"

August rolled his eyes, shrugged his shoulders, and seemed to come to terms with the loss of the most important tech he had ever created.

"Well, nothin' can be done about it now," he said. "We just have to move on from here, right? How's packin' goin', Sam?"

A change of subject was exactly what they needed, and she was glad August had done it before she could.

"Sweets, I ain't packing a thing," she said with a wicked grin. "We got enough Credit to buy whatever we need, wherever we go. Speaking of which, have you decided where we're going first?"

August's eyes beamed as he stood up, and walked over to the laundry basket. He picked out the dress that Samantha had worn yesterday; a very simple, knee-length, navy blue dress with white dots all over it.

"You gotta at least take this one dress, babe," he told her, holding the dress out to her.

Samantha looked at the limp article of clothing in her husband's hand and realized why he chose that one particular garment.

"You remember, sweets? How on Earth do you remember this dress, August?"

He let out a short laugh before pulling her close, and said, "When the lights went out that night, I wasn't scared. You know why? Somethin' felt right; somethin' close by. Then, when they all came back on, and I saw you for the first time, I knew that I would spend every minute of the rest of my life tryin' to get you to marry me. Of course I remember this dress. It was what you were wearing between the lanterns when we first met."

Samantha lay her head on August's chest and listened to the drum beat of his heart. It always sounded so loud, but it was a comforting rhythm. A teardrop fell from her eye, and she whispered to him, "Sweets, I love you so much… it hurts when you aren't holding me."

August kissed her gently and held onto her even tighter. After a silent moment, he said, "As for the first stop on the trip? I picked a place that I know you've always wanted to visit… your ancestral homeland, Sam: China. It's supposed to be magical but difficult all at the same time. There's a lot to do there, you know? Trace your family line back, and even find some relatives. Do some sightseeing. Visit the Great

Wall! See the panda memorials and where they used to live. What do you think?"

She couldn't speak. Breathless, light-headed, and with her eyes burning... Samantha's emotions overcame her. So she hugged her incredibly thoughtful husband as tight as she could, and cried into his shoulder.

August picked her up and carried her to the bedroom. After a little while, they made love gently and slowly. There was no rush. It was more about being with one another, and being a part of one another, than finishing. They lost themselves in each other and found a stronger bond than ever before. It was the most intimate and beautiful moment they ever shared together. But it would be the last time either of them ever had sex.

CHAPTER 22
DAY THREE

So far, today had been perfect for both Samantha and August. They had both woken still wrapped in the spell of the previous night's lovemaking; both still drunk on the power of that moment together.

They only spoke a few words here and there, preferring the silence of the early morning while they made breakfast together. Afterward, they just sat on opposite ends of the couch with their legs intertwined and read real books, made of real paper. August read a fantasy novel, as usual, and Samantha read an entertaining autobiography written by a hilarious female comedian. At lunchtime, they finally broke the silence with the sound of their grumbling stomachs.

"Sweets, I think our bellies are trying to tell us something," she said with a laugh.

August looked down at his stomach and shushed it, saying, "You can't tell me what to do, Steve."

Samantha arched an eyebrow at the man she had been with for years, and with a very curious tone said, "Steve? You... you named your stomach Steve?"

He merely shrugged his shoulders, tilted his head, and answered, "He never used to be big enough to have a name, but years of eatin' your cookin' have made him large and in charge. He's earned a formal title."

Samantha looked at him like August had lost his marbles and said, "And you went with Steve..."

"As good a name as any," he told her. "Now, despite what I just told Steve, he can actually tell me what to do, and often does. Let's fill him up. I'm thinkin' we can make some sandwiches and hit Poplar Head Park for a little picnic. What say you, wench?"

"Wench? Don't go using your fantasy novel lingo on me, sweets," she said, and then muttered under her breath, "What say you... I swear to the Lord above."

They laughed together, with their legs still intertwined on the couch. August got off of the sofa and bowed deeply, saying, "Verily, m'lady."

He was in the kitchen long before the book flew at him from his wife's perch.

After lunch, they took a walk down South Foster and over to West Main Street. They walked by where the diner used to be. Standing there, holding hands, they reminisced about days gone by. They talked about Tara, and how much Samantha missed her still. They spoke of the man who brought them together, John.

"He was so sweet in the diner that day," she recalled. "He was about to cry because he couldn't pay for his pie. Come to find out that he wanted it so bad because it was his ex-wife's recipe. I mean… how beautiful is that, sweets?"

August nodded and said, "Man, that old fella was somethin' else. It had been so long since I had met someone that kind. Not since my granny had passed, I guess."

"You know, if it hadn't been for Montek we might not have ended up together," Samantha regretfully admitted. "They put out the coupon, which brought both you and John to the diner that day."

August hated to admit it, but she was right. Montek did have a lot to do with their getting together.

"Yeah, that did get us to meet for the second time," he said begrudgingly. "But I think what truly brought us together was, and I hate to say it, but it was John's accident outside of the diner. When you called to tell me how he had been hit by an AutoCar and was in the clinic, and then asked me to be there with you to ease his passing? Well, I knew you were good inside. I wanted to be there for John, yeah, absolutely. But I wanted to be there with you, too."

Samantha looked into his bright eyes. He looked back and squeezed her hand forcefully.

"You're right, sweets," she said. "And then to find out he was Cheryl's ex-husband, and that he was giving the diner to me... and the house, too! It was fate. It was all destiny. God had a hand in everything. I just know it."

August sighed. He still wasn't sure if he believed in God. As an inventor, or tinkerer, he had made the SameSoul with science, and it was going to change the world very soon. Most people weren't very religious anymore, so August was certain a vast majority of the world would love to live forever inside of a robot. But Sam kept holding onto the belief that there was a Heaven, and that a soul should be free to move on. August didn't necessarily agree.

"Maybe, babe. Maybe he did," August said, not wanting to argue about faith in that perfectly beautiful moment.

"She, sweets," Sam said with a wink. "God is a woman."

Suddenly, August felt something hit him in the shoulder with the force of a truck. He spun around awkwardly to see an old lady walking by with a Montek.Automaton at her side. Her robot was what had clipped August so hard.

He listened as they talked to one another. It was a newer model, one that had his tech in it. Not the SameSoul, though. It was too soon for Montek to have gotten that into production. No, it was the improvements he had made to the body, voice systems, and BrainSave that he could detect just by watching and listening.

The body type was newer and more human-like, suspiciously looking like Woodrow 2.0. The voice sounded less robotic and more like this woman's husband. One of the innovations he had made was a vocal capture in the BrainSave that could emulate the deceased's voice based on a sample. And the way the automaton responded to the old woman; they were having a conversation. It was wonderful to see his work affecting someone in such a positive way. He didn't even mind his sore shoulder at that moment.

"Sam, do you see that?" he said, pointing to the old woman.

Samantha had not been paying attention to any of it and was still looking at the site of her old diner. Cheryl's old restaurant. She was still thinking of all the meals she had cooked inside, and all the wonderful smells that used to permeate this area because of that extraordinary old place. It was all gone now and had been for a while. But Samantha could still see it in her mind's eye.

"Hmm? What's that, sweets?" she answered dreamily, turning around to look at her husband, and letting go of his hand.

"That old lady and her automaton," he said, still pointing. "Ain't it great? That could be us one day, you know, only much better with the SameSoul. If only I could find the damn thing." Revisiting that frustration, he kicked at a loose stone on the ground... and fell.

Samantha grabbed at his hand, but it was no good. He fell right onto his ass. Hard. She covered her mouth to stifle a gasp, but when she saw the look on his face, Sam burst out laughing.

"Not funny, babe. I think I broke my coccyx," he said with a stifled laugh and a smile.

His wife laughed even harder now; bent over at the knees, gasping for air and tears streaming from her eyes.

August stood up, dusted off his jeans, and joined in the laughter, saying, "You know, Sam, I'm startin' to think you ain't as good-hearted as I once believed."

She tried to stop giggling to apologize, but couldn't stop.

"I'm…sorry…sweets. Oh my gosh," she somehow got out between laughs, "I needed that. Thank you."

August gave her a theatrical bow for the second time that day and said, "Happy to be of service, m'lady. Now why don't we head over to…" but he was interrupted as he stepped off of the curb, into the path of a fast-approaching AutoCar.

Samantha tried to stop him and failed once again.

"August! Look out!" she screamed.

The AutoCar passenger was reading a newspaper and letting the vehicle do the driving. It detected a new obstacle in its path, and moved to avoid August without slowing.

It was not enough.

The AutoCar slammed into him, not fully, but enough to send August flying into the road. He lay there bleeding and silent. The machine drove on, never even stopping.

CHAPTER 23
DAY FIVE

August woke suddenly. His heart was racing as he looked frantically from side to side, trying to figure out where the hell he was. The recognition wasn't instant, as his head was thick with pain and veiled in a mental fog. But August soon realized he was in the clinic on West Main Street. Recognition hit him as August saw one of the heartless nurses who let John die, years before. He even spared a moment to wonder why the man still worked here.

August was hooked up to several machines, and his arm lay at his side in a cast. He looked in the mirror mounted on the wall beside the bed, and saw that his face was a mess of scrapes and bruises. The rest of his body just about matched that look.

August glanced at the news vid playing on the monitor built into his bedtable and saw the date.

"Oh dear God, I've missed an entire day…"

Pulling at the lines in his arms and the tube in his nose, he called for a nurse. The other terrible nurse came striding into the room at the sound of the beeps from the machines, more than to August's calls.

"Patient Lurie, stop that. You're only making things worse. Just lie back and I'll drug you up so you can sleep," the nurse said.

August pushed the horrible man away from him, and yelled, "NO! Don't you dare put anythin' in me. You'll regret it if you do. Where is my wife?"

The nurse scrunched up his face and said, "Fine, I won't help you. You just go ahead and hurt yourself worse. I don't give a damn."

August grabbed at the rude man and yelled into his face, "WHERE IS MY WIFE?"

The nurse's face took on a look of fear as he backed away and tried to pry Patient Lurie's strong hands from his scrubs.

"Who? I mean, what... what does she look like? Maybe I saw her," the nurse stammered pleadingly.

"She's a Chinese woman, Southern accent, long, black hair... calls everyone sweets," August said, describing the love of his life.

The nurse's eyes opened wider in recognition and even rolled a little before thinking better of it, as he said, "Oh, her. She's been storming around the clinic for a whole day now, talking to everyone who will listen about waking her husband up. I guess that's you. Well, I saw her leaving about an hour ago. Probably, your wife just wants to change clothes and shower. She's been here for too damn long if you ask my opinion."

August let go of the man's scrubs, who then fell back a few steps as a result.

"I didn't ask your opinion," he told the wretched nurse. "Now get out of my way. I'm going home. I'll be back later to sign any paperwork."

The nurse started to protest, but at a glare from August he just nodded in agreement and left the room in a hurry.

Getting home wasn't exactly easy for August. He had just been hit by an AutoCar two days ago and had suffered a broken arm and two ribs, not to mention the cuts and bruises covering the rest of him.

He had done his best to change back into his own clothes, but they weren't in the best condition, and neither was he. The result was a shirt buttoned improperly, which created a very crooked appearance. That coupled with the blood on the garment made him look frightful. His pants were on, but August couldn't find his belt, so he had one hand holding them up, the other hand held his shoes. There were no socks either.

August had no idea how he was going to get home, but knew he needed to see his wife as soon as possible. He began hobbling down the street in the direction of their home.

"You look terrible, Mr. Lurie," a familiar voice said.

August glanced to the side and saw Joshua Stevens had just pulled up next to him in an AutoCar.

"I feel it, too, Mr. Stevens," August admitted. "Look, I need a ride to my house. Could you please give me a lift? I'd greatly appreciate it."

Mr. Stevens eyed the bloody clothes and almost said no, but August had just made Joshua a very rich man, so he didn't especially care about the interior of this AutoCar. He was going to buy a new and more luxurious one tomorrow.

"Get in, Mr. Lurie," he said without question.

August went to open the passenger side door, but hesitated and said, "Before I get in, tell me one thing. Did you steal my SameSoul prototype?"

Joshua looked aghast and said, "Why the hell would I do that? You sold us the blueprints. I can just make one now; I don't need yours."

"Damn," August said to himself, deciding to worry about it later.

Right now he needed to get home to Sam.

He got into the car, slammed the door shut, and said to Mr. Stevens, "Drive. Fast."

They pulled up to the Lurie family home soon after, and August exited the car without a word to Joshua Stevens.

"Goodbye, Mr. Lurie," he called after August.

The AutoCar peeled off, going way too fast for this street. He should probably slow down. There were kids in this neighborhood.

August tore open the front door and started yelling out for his wife, "Sam! Are you here? Babe?" He ran to every door and threw them open, shouting all the while, "Sam! Babe! I'm home! Where are you?"

August hoped he hadn't missed her. He hoped she wasn't headed back to the clinic while he was on the way here. If she was, how would he get back? August couldn't ride a bike in this condition. He sat down on the couch to catch his breath, starting to feel woozy from all the physical activity. He closed his eyes for just a moment, and the lanterns automatically dimmed their light.

He woke to the sound of the doorbell.

Shit! He had fallen asleep. It wasn't his fault; August was still in immense amounts of pain as the meds were wearing off, and his body was trying to help.

The doorbell rang again.

August struggled to his feet and made his way to the front door. The lanterns followed him.

"Sam! Is that you?" he called out, as he pulled the door open as quickly as he could in this wounded state. Standing there was not his wife, but a man in a white coat.

"Dr. Granger?" August asked, his voice full of confusion. "What are you doin' here? Look, I'm real sorry I left without fillin' out the proper paperwork; it's just that I needed to find my wife. You understand, right?"

Dr. Granger shrugged his shoulders as if he didn't care and said, "We've got all of your information on file, Patient Lurie. Your leaving the clinic so soon won't deprive me of my payment. I'll get it, don't you worry about that. I'm here to give you this."

Dr. Granger handed over a large envelope with a bulge in the bottom, and August accepted it curiously.

"What is it, doc?" he asked.

"I know you and your wife don't seem to think so," Dr. Granger said, aggravated, "but I'm a very busy man. I don't normally do stuff like this, but she paid me an exorbitant amount of money to deliver this package to you and to… perform other duties that I'm sure will be detailed inside that envelope."

With that, Dr. Granger turned around and walked to the street where he had parked his AutoCar. August, standing on the front doorstep in between the lanterns, was at a loss for words momentarily.

When he found them, August called out, "Dr. Granger, you were with my wife today? Where is she? Is she back at the clinic?"

The "good" doctor didn't even slow his stride or turn around.

"No," Dr. Granger called back over his shoulder. "She's dead."

CHAPTER 24
I'M SORRY

She's dead? What the hell was Dr. Granger talking about? The nurse had said she was just at the clinic this morning.

"Doc! Doc! What do you mean?" August screamed after him, hobbling as fast as he could to reach the AutoCar just before it pulled away.

The "good" doctor rolled down the window looking irritated, and said, "Just open the envelope and read the letter inside, Patient Lurie. Then get back to the clinic as soon as you can so we can clean you up. You don't want to get an infection. Or maybe you do. I don't care."

He peeled off faster than he should on this street. He should probably slow down. There were children in this neighborhood.

August sat down on the front lawn and tore open the large envelope. Inside there were two items and a letter. He ignored everything else and pulled the handwritten note out, and as he read the first two lines, he began to wail mournfully, tears falling from his eyes like a heavy rain.

August. My love. I'm sorry. I ached to tell you before, but I didn't want to spoil your plans. I didn't want us to spend our last few days together in sadness. They have been wonderful days, haven't they? You see, my Countdown started five days ago...

Suddenly, August stopped reading and stood up angrily. Still crying, and with a shattered heart, he could barely breathe with the agony inside of his chest. But he was also pissed beyond belief.

"How could you do this to me, Sam?!" he screamed into the night. "You know what I went through with Granny! YOU KNEW IT! Now I gotta go through it all over again, and this time, it's worse! WHY? Why did you do this?"

He fell back to his knees and sobbed on all fours. A sudden wave of nausea swept over him, and August threw up in the grass. He heard voices and saw that a few neighbors had heard his yells and were staring at him from their front doors. Not wanting to continue reading the letter here and now, he stood up and stumbled back inside, slamming the door behind him, and feeling lost. This house wasn't his home anymore; not without Sam. It seemed like some strange, foreign land to him, when suddenly he felt very sick again and ran to the toilet.

After composing himself somewhat, August went into the bedroom and sat on the bed. The covers were still down from the last time they had woken together. He reached out and touched her pillow. Fresh tears fell from his eyes and he found the strength to read more of the letter.

I had been sick with stomach cancer, but Dr. Granger cured it and repaired all the damage the disease had caused inside of me. It was after that, when everything was back to normal, that he found the Countdown. I kept it all from you to spare your feelings. I didn't want you to worry.

August stopped again and covered his face with his hands. She had kept it from him to spare his feelings... just like his granny had done... just like he had kept his worries and feelings from Sam the past few days. It was like God was punishing him for not being honest.

"Oh, so now I believe in God?" August asked himself sarcastically. "Now that I need someone to blame? I can't believe this is happenin'. What am I going to do without you, Sam? I can't... I just can't..." He trailed off and read on.

I didn't want you to worry. I know that sounds stupid, sweets. And I know that you're probably cursing my name right about now. I hate that I'm doing to you what your granny did. It's not my intention to make you go through that again. But it's my death. My life. I didn't want to spend the last few days of it lying around crying about our lost future. I wanted to spend those precious last few days making love to you, and reading on the couch with you, and having a picnic with you. Those memories will stay with me in Heaven forever.

August threw down the unfinished letter and paced the room. He was alone... utterly alone. Forever. She had left him. It wasn't her fault, but that didn't change anything. If August was being honest with himself, he could see why she did it this way. It was her choice; she was right about that. Her life, and her death. It didn't make this hurt any less for him, though. He picked up the letter again.

Those memories will stay with me in Heaven forever. But Heaven might just have to wait. You don't have to be alone, sweets. I've given you a choice. Inside the envelope are two boxes. One of them is my ashes. Take them and spread them wherever you travel, all over the world. Leave a part of me everywhere you go. Or you could choose the other box. It's your SameSoul prototype. I'm in it.

August dropped the letter this time and dove for the envelope. He plunged his hand inside and pulled out a box containing his wife's remains. He stared at it for a long minute, before kissing it and placing it on the dresser. "I love you, babe," he whispered.

He reached back in and pulled out the other box; the SameSoul. The one he had thought lost or stolen for days. One of the reasons he had been in such a bad mood recently, and Samantha had it the whole time.

"Damn it, woman," he muttered. August stared at the SameSoul and rolled it around in his hands. Then he picked up the letter to finish reading it.

I'm in it. If you want me to be with you for longer, just call Woodrow, and he'll come. I've dressed him in a few of my old things. You know what to do from there. It's your decision, sweets. I've given you a choice because you are my everything. I have loved you more than anyone has ever loved someone else. I've loved you more than scientifically or spiritually possible. I have loved you, August, my tinkerer, my life, my one and only. I still love you and will always love you. I'll see you at some point soon; either through the eyes of an automaton or at the Pearly Gates waiting to embrace you. Goodbye, sweets.

And that was it. Nothing more. August had to decide whether to let her go to Heaven, which he knew she wanted, but he wasn't even sure if it existed or not, or to put her into Woodrow, which would be selfish and was something he knew Samantha didn't want.

How could he possibly make that choice? August took the box containing her ashes from the dresser and opened it. Inside was another sealed container, but this one was translucent. He could now see what remained of his wife.

"But those are only her physical remains," he thought.

In his other hand was her essence. Her consciousness. He could talk to her right now. His wife was the only person who could make August feel better. August could tell her how much it hurt not to have her here. He wanted to tell Samantha how much he loved her right then.

"Woodrow! Woodrow," he called out loudly. "Get in here! Woodrow!"

August immediately heard the sound of clacking wood coming down the hallway. It rattled like the unrolling of a wooden plank bridge.

Woodrow stepped into the room, and the sight initially made August laugh; until he remembered the significance of the wooden automaton's appearance. Woodrow had on a baseball cap that August had given to Samantha a few years ago, which said, "Kiss the Cook" on it. The automaton was also wearing Samantha's wedding and engagement rings on a chain around its neck. But most importantly, Woodrow wore a navy blue dress with white dots all over it.

The sight of that dress sent August into a fit of sobbing again, and he fell onto the bed; burying his face in Samantha's pillow, breathing in the smell of her hair. It was faint, and August knew it would only grow weaker every single day. Soon, he would forget the distinct scent of his wife's long black hair. His favorite fragrance in the world was now gone forever, and so he greedily inhaled the last remnants.

At that moment, August seemed to make up his mind. He grabbed the SameSoul and walked over to Woodrow. The automaton already knew what to do, and opened the port created for a BrainSave that would now house a much more advanced tech, one that August had designed and built.

Woodrow reached out his wooden hand and took the little box from August. Without missing a beat, the automaton raised its hand and began to place the chip in the receiver port.

"I'm sorry," August whimpered.

He then reached out lightning-fast, and slapped the SameSoul out of Woodrow's hand, sending it flying across the room.

CHAPTER 25
LET GO

The SameSoul soared across the room, and August immediately chased after it, his face a mask of fear. Before it could collide with the ground and possibly damage the consciousness of the woman within, he cupped his hands around the small data module and delicately plucked it from the air.

A large sigh escaped his lips as he opened his hands and saw the undamaged box held there. Looking over at Woodrow, who was now walking towards August and the SameSoul, August realized the automaton wasn't done trying to implant the device yet.

"Woodrow," he said in warning, "back off now, buddy. I've changed my mind. I don't want to install this just yet."

"IN STALL," the human-like wooden automaton wearing a navy blue dress, baseball cap, and necklace replied as it reached out for the SameSoul.

Woodrow tried to take the data box from August, but met resistance; August wouldn't let go. He couldn't let go.

"Stop it now, Woodrow," August ordered his creation. "I... I'm... I don't think I can do it. She wouldn't want this."

This time, the automaton heeded the commands given to it by the sole remaining creator. Woodrow stopped trying to take the SameSoul. He turned around and trundled to the corner where he powered down, the port for the SameSoul still open and waiting.

August scooped up the box containing Samantha's ashes from the dresser. He took only that and the vessel containing his wife's consciousness with him as he left their home and locked it up, planning on never returning, and took out his cell phone.

"Hello?" a voice weary with sleep said over the Montek.Communication line.

August glanced at the time and wondered why on Earth his old friend, and the Best Man at his wedding, was doing still asleep at this hour of the day.

"Bobby, hi. It's August," he replied into his cellphone.

Bobby Li cleared his throat and August heard the sound of a cigarette being lit. Some people still clung to bad habits, even in today's medically advanced world.

"Dude. What's up? I was sleeping real hard. Had a late gig last night, you know. Shitty tips, too. So, what's happening, man? Haven't talked to you in, like, four months."

"Yeah, sorry about the lack of contact," August said, trying his best to hold it together, but audibly struggling.

"I wanted…" he choked on his words and held back a full-blown wail, leaving him unable to speak for a moment.

"August, you ok?" Bobby asked, concern touching the edges of his tired voice. "What's the matter?"

He seemed genuinely concerned, which wasn't all that surprising. He may be a product of the modern world, but Bobby was a lot better than most people. It's one of the reasons August had always stayed friends with him. No matter what, Bobby would always be there to help. He may be late, he may be rude about it, but unlike most people alive today, he would never say no to a friend in need.

"It's Sam," August breathed quietly into the cellphone. "Bobby… she's dead."

"What? How? When?" Bobby asked all in a rush. "August, I'm so sorry. Where are you?"

August thought about telling him, so they could meet up somewhere. Seeing a friendly face might offer some comfort, and asking Bobby for this favor in person would be the polite thing to do. But honestly, August felt like he would never be happy again, and seeing Bobby at this point would only drag out the process, keeping August in New Dothan longer than he wanted.

"Listen, Bobby… I need your help," August said with difficulty. "I'm… I'm leavin' town, and probably never comin' back."

Bobby was silent for a breath or two, before he said, "Ok, I get it, man. So, like now? Are you gone? Right now?"

"Yeah… as soon as I can," August replied. "But… I can't let go of our house, Bobbo. I need you to… take care of it for me. I don't want you to live in it or nothin'… just go there a couple of times a month, you know? Maybe pay a cleanin' service to keep it livable. Like I said, I'll probably never come back, but nothin' is ever guaranteed. I learned that today."

Bobby blew out a long breath, probably along with a large cloud of cigarette smoke, and said, "Man, of course I'll help. But I'm like, you know, barely making ends meet as it is right now. I can't afford a cleaning service. Sorry, dude. I mean, I can clean it myself if you want me to, though."

August shook his head, even though Bobby couldn't see him. His hands were shaking, too, he realized. He sat down on the curb, realizing for the first time that he was probably in shock. With his injuries still very fresh, and the loss of his entire world, it was a reasonably certain condition.

"No man, I'll take care of the Credit. I've sold somethin' to Montek… somethin' big. They paid me real well. If you keep up the house for me, I'll drop enough Credit in your account to pay for the cleanin' and for you to live on. Call it a good-bye present from an old friend. You won't have to worry about makin' ends meet anymore, man."

Bobby was lost for words. He stumbled through a few un-intelligible syllables several times before finally finding his voice as he replied, "August, I can't take your Credit, man. I mean, unless you really want me to. I could use it."

"It's done," August said, glad to have this taken care of. "I'll set you up, brother. I love you, Bobbo. Thanks for helpin' me out... it means the world to me. I'll be in contact some-time to check in."

"Hey, no worries," Bobby Li replied. "And don't thank me, I should be thanking you." He paused on the line, and then in a heartbroken voice added, "I am sorry about Samantha. I'm sure you don't wanna talk about it right now, but when you do... please call me, Auggie. Where are you going?"

August thought for a moment. He didn't really care where he was going. The tickets were already booked to Shanghai for him, Woodrow, and Sam. Of course, there was no way August was taking Woodrow now. He would just have to travel alone.

"Yeah, you're right: I don't want to talk about it now," August replied. "Just know she didn't suffer. It was the Count-down that got her... just like Granny. I'm uh... I guess I'm going to China."

Bobby nodded his head, even though August couldn't see him. It made sense for him to visit Sam's motherland. Bobby had more that he wanted to say, but he didn't really know how to express those thoughts and feelings. Being a writer of music, Bobby had beautiful prose he could tap into at a moment's notice. But the loss of life had been such a normal and humdrum thing for so long, most people didn't get too worked up over it anymore, including Bobby.

But this felt different somehow. The love he witnessed between August and Samantha had been unique. In his lifetime, Bobby had never seen two people blend so perfectly. Her death actually broke Bobby's heart, to his surprise.

"Listen… don't… don't worry about the house," Bobby said, now the one fighting back tears. "I'll make sure it's ready for you, should you ever come back. And if you don't, I'll preserve all the memories you two shared in there. You just… you just go, man. Get out of here and start a new life. I know it hurts… hell, it hurts me, so I can't imagine how bad it hurt for you… But your new life is ready to begin. Even if you don't want it… it's out there. Just let go."

August was crying harder than ever at hearing these words from Bobby, who had never expressed such emotion in all the years August had known him. He couldn't even say goodbye to his old friend. August just pressed the end button on his cellphone.

–

Using his new wealth and resources, August ended up in Birmingham later that day and checked into a hospital. He wanted to heal up properly before heading to China, and his wounds were still fresh from the accident with the AutoCar. The hospital in Birmingham was new and had the best healing tech in all of Alabama. It was top of the line, and August could afford that now.

August spent two days subjecting himself to the most expensive treatments available to mend his bones, and heal his cuts and scrapes. There was no pain, as the hospital staff was incredible in their profession. And best of all, in August's opinion, they weren't the personnel of the Granger Clinic on West Main Street.

After those two days, he spent a week wandering around, exploring Birmingham. After all, August had never left New Dothan, so he was curious about the biggest city in Alabama. He found that it was just like his home town, only a little larger with a few more tall buildings, a few more parks, and a few more restaurants. The automated sidewalks moved at the same speed, and he avoided them just the same as he always had back home. They even used the same lanterns as in New Dothan.

Seeing them, and with memories flooding into his mind, August fell to his knees in the middle of the street in downtown Birmingham. He wailed at the memory of his first meeting with Samantha between the lanterns on West Main Street. August couldn't handle the pain. He couldn't take the constant reminders of his wife. He had to get out of Alabama. He had to leave North America. The United States of Earth covered the whole planet, and he could go anywhere. It was time to leave. He had to let go.

CHAPTER 26
NEW LIFE

One month later, August was walking through the rice fields in a rural Chinese village near Guilin. He had set up a base for himself in the city of Chengdu and ventured out from there for days at a time.

August left all his tech at the apartment in Chengdu. He had chosen that city based on recommendations from locals in Shanghai, who said Chengdu had great food that was very spicy. Having no idea what was in store for him anywhere in this enormous and foreign land, August blindly trusted them and was glad he had done so.

It was shocking to see almost no other skin color than that of his recently dead wife. At first, it felt like the worst idea in the world to have come here to escape constant reminders of Sam. But everything else was so different, that the only distraction was the locals' skin and hair. None of them were as beautiful as she was in his eyes, so he didn't care.

Now, August was quite a local celebrity wherever he went. Despite the world having only one government, and with the advent of free Internet and wifi in every little village in the world, China still held onto its ancient culture with iron grips. So it was no surprise that he was the first black man that many of the local villagers had ever seen.

They all, especially the elderly and the children, wanted to feel his skin and touch his hair. August didn't mind, though. It was like being loved by someone again. Having them caress his arms and face, or press at his hair — even pulling at it sometimes — he could close his eyes and imagine it was Samantha.

Since coming to China, he had decided that letting go of her was impossible. Instead, what August desperately needed to do was accept his loss. Embrace the love they had shared, because it would sustain him. Sadness visited August almost every day, but he chose to find new ways each time to take his mind somewhere different, to a fearless and positive place.

Sometimes he helped the local farmers with their manual labor. Other times, he sat down and wrote about how he was feeling at that very moment. Mostly, though, when the feeling of sadness came over him so strongly August felt he would suffocate... that was when he cooked.

August would stop into the nearest restaurant or café, or sometimes even someone's home, and offer him or her a large amount of Credit if they would teach him to cook something new. Every time he smelled the warm aroma of food cooking, and it was his hands doing some of the work, August filled with radiant energy; an almost... magical feeling.

His logical mind told him it was happiness. He was happy because he was doing something of which the woman he gave his heart to forever would approve. At the back of his mind, though, he always thought it was Sam. That she was there guiding his hands and helping him make these unusual and unbelievably delectable local dishes you would never find on a menu back home in a million years. A Nutricator couldn't even begin to manufacture dishes this intricate.

Nutricators... Every time he saw one, August thought of how much Samantha had hated those. And he saw them everywhere in China, of course. They were mandatory in all homes. But many of the homes out in these local villages opted to use it to feed livestock. They would make pig feed with one of Montek's Nutricators, and then once the pigs were fat and ready, they would slaughter the pigs and make real food. Samantha would have loved it.

It was one such day that a great idea, a real spark of inspiration, came to August. An idea that would set him forth on a new course, his new life. Because what he was doing now, it wasn't long-term. It was intermediate. It was all just a space filler. August was merely learning how to adjust to his life without Samantha, but that wouldn't be enough, and he knew it. August would need to do something important again.

He had been walking down the street in this village, when a Montek.Automaton advertisement caught his eye. It was the first one he had seen since selling the SameSoul to the global mega-conglomerate. This ad was announcing Montek's newest and greatest innovation.

ARE YOU AFRAID OF DEATH? DO YOU WANT TO LIVE FOREVER? WELL, THANKS TO THE GREAT MINDS AT MONTEK... NOW YOU CAN! ANNOUNCING THE NEWEST AND MOST SIGNIFICANT INNOVATION IN HUMAN HISTORY: NewLife. AS A REPLACEMENT FOR THE BrainSave, THIS MARVEL OF TECHNOLOGY WILL IMPLANT YOUR CONSCIOUSNESS INTO A MONTEK.AUTOMATON SO THAT YOU CAN GO ON LIVING AFTER YOU DIE. VISIT US ON THE WEB OR STOP BY YOUR LOCAL MONTEK.AUTOMATON DEALER FOR MORE DETAILS.

Reading this, August only rolled his eyes and continued walking to his destination.

Later, August stood in a little old woman's home as she showed him how to make a recipe she had inherited from her mother, who had inherited it from hers, and on and on further back down their family tree.

She spoke excellent English, but many of the ingredients she chose to call by their Chinese names because that was how the recipe was written. So August ended up not knowing specifically every component that went into the dish, but the electric feeling was there, and so he was happy.

"I wish more people would want to learn how to cook the old way, as you do, Nephew," the old woman said to him.

All the old Chinese people called him nephew for some reason, well either that or laowai – which meant foreigner. He never asked why, August just accepted it.

"Auntie, why don't they want to learn? I understand that in the big cities people are so obsessed with technology to the point of eating synthetic food for every meal, just like in my home town. But out here there's not a ton of tech, but instead so much nature. It seems like people would need to learn how to cook like this."

As the old woman continued cutting garlic and ginger, August took up a knife and joined her, making sure to match the size of his slices to hers.

"Unfortunately, Nephew," she replied, "every generation gets less and less interested in this. They all want to eat the disgusting fake food from those devils at Montek."

August grinned widely at that. It reminded him so much of his late wife, in a good way. That tingling feeling inside even intensified briefly.

"Well, I think it's important to grow real food, cook real food, and eat real food. I just can't stand eatin' Nutricator garbage anymore. It turns my stomach."

The old woman put her knife down and wiped her hands on the apron she wore around her waist. Her smile crinkled that old face up even more than the sun and time itself had done already.

"I agree. So, instead of you paying me to teach you this recipe, Nephew, I think you should spend that Credit on teaching others how to cook it," she proposed. "Set up in town and the young people will flock to the dark stranger. I think you might be able to convince some of them to change their way of thinking."

August dropped the knife, and his face went slack. Why hadn't he thought of this before? What better way to pay homage to the greatest person August had ever known — the love of his life. He was incredibly wealthy. He could make a difference in the world again.

Excitedly, August wiped his hands on his pants to remove the remnants of food, and bent down to kiss the old lady on both cheeks. "Thank you, Auntie," he said, barely able to contain his glee. "That is an excellent idea, but a little bit small for my likin'. I'm gonna have to take it to the next level. I'm gonna give the *whole world* a new life!"

He took off running out of her house without another word, ignoring her calls to get back and finish what he had started.

It was a few weeks later when the first Samantha's Place opened its doors. In thanks to the little old woman, he had started his idea in the very same small village where she lived. August had taken her idea and evolved it into a way to help people everywhere. Samantha's Place was a school, café, and farm. People could come in and learn how to farm real food, cook real food, and eat for free at the restaurant. Using the Credit just sitting in his bank account to fund these all over the world was going to be August and Samantha's legacy.

There was buzz all over social media about what he was doing here, and also what he was planning on doing after he left this village. And this was only the first location! On opening day, there were hundreds of people waiting, which was a lot in this remote location, but August knew it would grow. This place would help create a new and better life for these people, and everyone on Earth if he worked hard enough.

Six years after he opened the first Samantha's Place in rural China, August was proven right. Since the first location, August had spread out. There were hundreds of Samantha's Place locations in China now. And more importantly, they were all self-sufficient after the initial start-up costs he funded with the money he had made from selling the SameSoul to Montek.

August would choose a place with a local population that needed help and also had enough arable land nearby to make it a viable candidate. He then funded the projects and even oversaw the first dozen or so locations all the way from breaking ground until each site was no longer in need of his funding. After the first dozen Samantha's Places, he started hiring and training people to set them up for him, so that August was free to scout future sites.

Samantha's Place was famous the world over now, and other areas were begging for August's help. They all wanted to be a part of his vision.

August was splitting his time between Thailand, Vietnam, Malaysia, and Indonesia. Over 30 sites were being set up all over Southeast Asia as he spoke on his same old cellphone to Bobby Li while walking through a field in rural Thailand.

"But why Southeast Asia only, man?" Bobby asked. "Why not head west? Help Old Europe out! They need an intervention, dude. Just last week I saw a vid clip on the news from Vatican City where they had the world's largest Nutri-cator continually making food for the poor. They should be eating your real food, man, not that slop."

August laughed at the thought of Bobby's transformation over the past six years. When August had left Alabama, the poor musician Bobby was a Nutricator advocate, his diet consisting solely of Nutricator sweet tea and Nutricator fried chicken. Once August had made a large enough impact on the world with his Samantha's Place idea, he had flown Bobby out and trained him to run a location. After that, Bobby had a new life.

He returned to New Dothan and set up a site in Headland Town. The farmers there were very welcoming of the help and combined all of their farms together, and it was now one of the world's largest Samantha's Places.

"We'll get there, Bobbo. I promise, buddy," August told his old friend. "So, is everythin' goin' ok with the house?"

Bobby exhaled loudly, probably blowing an enormous cloud of cigarette smoke.

"Great, dude. Holly is still keeping the place clean once a month. She's amazing. I've got her cleaning my place, too. Though the other day she tried to clean Woodrow and it… uh… powered on and told her to MOVE AWAY or some-thing like that. Scared the shit out of her, dude."

They both laughed at that. August hadn't thought of Wood-row in a couple of years. He was busy with his new life and had forgotten about the old hunk of wood. Now that Bobby had mentioned Woodrow, though, August felt an empty hole in his heart. He missed the automaton, as weird as that was. Of course, it all had to do with how much August still missed Sam. Suddenly, he felt the need to cook something, and very soon.

They chatted about how the Headland Town location was doing, but August didn't pay much attention. He trusted his old friend to run things, and August couldn't show too much interest in one location or he'd stop for too long and never get moving again. The constant movement... even six years later... helped him stay focused and not fall into depression.

As he walked along the roadside heading back to the small village, August added a few noises of agreement in response to Bobby once in a while. He walked by a little shop near the edge of town that had all kinds of different lamps, lights, and maglev lanterns in the shop window. There was no signage to indicate what they sold, or why, but it was obvious this was your go-to place for lighting in this small, rural town. Looking in the window, August noticed something. Right there, on the top shelf at eye level, were two of his LifeLan-terns.

With no idea whatsoever how they could have possibly made it all the way to Thailand, he abruptly ended the call with Bobby and promised to call him back later. August quickly entered the shop and took the two lanterns off of the shelf.

"Excuse me, do you know where these came from?" he asked the shop owner.

The young man was a very tall and skinny Thai hipster, part of the retro movement that somehow still held sway in this part of the world. Retro these days, though, was considered of things only slightly out of date. The new stuff hit the shelves, and all the sheep rushed out to buy, buy, buy. The hipsters then swooped in and got the older models reasonably cheap.

The shop owner eyed the Life Lanterns and nodded his head, saying, "Yeah, kap. I think this guy sold them to me about a year ago, kap. He said it was a pair from somewhere in North America...Alabama, maybe... Yeah, it was Alabama, kap."

"Unbelievable," August said under his breath. "I mean...to come all this way..."

"Hey, man, you got Credit?" the man asked brusquely. "If not, put it back and leave."

August didn't even ask how much. He just pulled out his cellphone and accessed the Montek.Credit app. He still refused to have a SmartChip implanted. As usual, he was met with a shocked look, quickly followed by an uncaring shrug.

The purchase finalized, August headed back out the street and called Bobby back to ask for a favor. Seeing these lanterns had reminded August of his and Samantha's lanterns back in their house... and everything that had happened between them.

"Damn, August. That was fast," Bobby said, only half-kidding. "You never call back so soon. I wasn't expecting to hear from you for another month or two."

"Yeah, well. Shut it, man," August said, admitting to himself that Bobby was right, and making a mental note to call his old friend more often. "Listen, Bobby, I need your help again. You know the lanterns from mine and Sam's weddin'? The ones you helped out with before? Are they still in the house?"

Bobby blew some smoke, and cleared his throat, replying, "Yeah, man. They're still floating around waiting for orders."

August did a victory fist pump in the middle of the street. A few people looked at him as if he were insane, but he ignored their stares. The lanterns still worked, which was fantastic news, as he had something in mind for them.

"I need you to take them somewhere for me," August said. "They need a new life... or to revisit an old one, I guess."

CHAPTER 27
WENT OUT

"It was 30 years ago today," he whispered to himself. An entire lifetime, it seemed to August. He had traveled the entire globe and started farming communities and cooking schools. He had provided free food to anyone in those communities who contributed in any way. He started a global movement towards real food. Earth still only had one government, but all of the old countries still existed, their borders were just a little blurrier now. But the customs and cultural differences mostly remained. August had visited all of these countries, and almost every single one had, at least, a few Samantha's Places, and most countries had many of them. Everywhere you found good farmland and people to feed, Samantha's Place was there, too.

August had made the world a better place. He had made a difference. He had lived his dream of traveling the world. Montek, unfortunately, still held sway with the government, but ten years back they had changed the laws concerning

Nutricators, finally. They were no longer mandatory the world over, and, in fact, had become so unpopular, Montek now marketed them as a cheap way to feed livestock.

Now the NewLife, on the other hand – Montek's version of the SameSoul – had blown up... but in a way that August honestly felt was positive. At first, everyone bought them. They were afraid to die because they were scared there would be nothing after this life. So in the first ten years after the NewLife entered the market, the population of the Earth went to about 70% human and 30% automatons. Realizing that this was going to be a problem soon, the "good" people at Montek contacted August and asked him to help them come up with a solution. He only said three words before disconnecting the call.

"Stop selling them."

That didn't seem to suit Montek, as they enjoyed making money way too much. So instead, their solution was to raise the price. Make it affordable only to the extremely wealthy. This plan worked somewhat, reducing the number of new units hitting the streets by over half.

It wasn't until five years later – 15 years after their intro-duction to the market – that the oldest NewLife inhabitants began to experience something strange. A tugging at their souls was what they described experiencing; a feeling of not being where they were supposed to be. This sensation seemed to point to a great beyond in many people's opinions, and many of the Montek.Automatons housing NewLife clients took their data module out and crushed it, sending their consciousness onward to whatever was next.

Now, 30 years later, Montek didn't even sell NewLife modules or Montek.Automatons anymore, because most people were now certain there was an afterlife. Citizens of the United States of Earth weren't scared of death anymore, and so they stopped buying the automatons and NewLife modules. And once they stopped buying, Montek stopped selling. It didn't matter that the feeling described by the NewLife automaton inhabitants was by no means irrefutable proof of Heaven or Hell. People only needed a tiny bit of reassurance that there might be something else beyond this life. It was enough.

There were a few very famous "people" still holding on and living forever in their automatons, but in the whole world, there were only 23 units still functioning.

August felt proud of all that he had done in his life and all that he had accomplished. He was even proud that the SameSoul had led to the NewLife, because that eventually led people to accept death instead of being afraid and trying to stop it from ever happening. It was all because of Samantha. He had done everything in her memory.

August hadn't gone around saying it was all for her or that she was his inspiration. She wouldn't have liked to be in the limelight like that. No, when asked who the Samantha of Samantha's Place was, August said it was his wife who had passed away from the Countdown, and that she had taught him about the importance of real food.

Despite not singing her praises to the whole world every waking moment, the way he wanted to, everything he had ever done over the past 30 years was because of Samantha, whom he still missed every day... whom he still loved with every single ounce of his heart and soul. And today, on the 30th anniversary of her death, August stood on their front lawn.

He had not been back in Alabama since he left all those years ago. The last time he had seen this house was the day that Samantha had passed away; the day he had woken in the Granger Clinic after being hit by an AutoCar. His arm still twinged from time to time where it had been broken, especially now that he was in his sixties.

August still had his keys. He had kept them in his pocket every day since he locked the door for the last time... in case August ever decided to come back all of a sudden. And he had thought about it a few times.

When the laws changed about Nutricators, knowing that he had made it happen, and knowing that Sam had also had a hand in it through him... August had thought to come here.

But he never did. August had come to believe in God over the years. He wasn't religious or anything; August never went to church. But he felt that something was connecting him with Samantha.

Every time he cooked and felt that electrical buzzing inside his chest, he knew she was with him. It wasn't just being happy or remembering the exultant feeling of being wildly in love. It was Sam. He knew it. He didn't need to ask her to find out the truth… but he might, anyway.

August stepped through the front door and received a wave of emotion upon looking at all of their worldly possessions in the same places where he left them. It wasn't sadness that swept over him at that moment, but rather elation at finally coming home, and a tremendous sense of relief that everything was as it should be. What had Sam said to him when they discussed whether or not to keep the house?

"When you need to feel comforted, where do you go? If you ever feel completely out of sorts and lost, the best place to go is always home."

And so, all these years later, when he felt out of sorts and in need of comforting… when he felt lost… August had come home to Alabama.

He reached into his pocket and pulled out something else he had been carrying in there for 30 years, and it was almost empty. There was only a pinch of Sam's ashes left. He took half of the bag and sprinkled it on the couch, exactly where she had been the last time they had lain there, reading together with their legs intertwined.

He smiled, but also let a tear fall down his cheek. It was the first time he had cried in years. It wasn't a tear of sorrow, but one that acknowledged the hole he still felt in his heart without Samantha beside him.

Next, August went to his workshop. He grabbed a few tools, which he put into the bag he had brought with him, which already contained a few containers of liquid. The tools and fluids all had one thing in common. They were used specifically for the upkeep, maintenance, and repair of wood.

-

Bobby had passed away several years ago. Too much smoking. Just because the medical community had cured cancer didn't mean that it had also cured emphysema. A year before he died, Bobby had come to visit August at the little bungalow in Malaysia where he had settled due to falling in love with the food. The food in Malaysia was life-altering.

During this visit, they had talked about life and love. Bobby had finally married Holly, the lady who cleaned August's house. They had made some kids together, who were all grown and out of the house by the time Bobby visited Malaysia to see his old friend.

"Bobby, have you gone to see them?" August asked, his voice touched with worry. "Are they still there? Are they still workin'?"

Bobby laughed, which caused a severe coughing fit, and replied, "You always ask about those damn things, Auggie. I mean, I get it. I do. And to answer your question, yes, I saw them a month ago, and they are still working fine."

August leaned back in his chair, the tension easing from his shoulders as he said, "Good. That's good. And you need to have that cough looked at, Bobbo. It don't sound too good."

Bobby hacked a little more nasty goo from his chest, and wheezed scarily for a moment before, waving August's worries away with both hands.

"Holly always says that shit, too," Bobby admitted. "I'm alright, man. I'll outlive you all. But, uh, August, you should know something. Most everything in New Dothan has switched to solar power, man. Tesla generators are ancient history now, you know, dude? Solar energy tech has leaped way ahead, and they've got it to where you can power a whole city for a month from an array the size of a football field."

August shot forward in his seat once more, eyes wild with worry, hands reaching for Bobby's, and said, "But they didn't tear down the generator outside of town, did they? I bought it years ago, you know! They can't tear it down. It's still working, too, right?"

Bobby pulled his hands away and wiped them on his pants, as if wiping off some errant crazy left there by his old friend, and replied, "Man, yes. Jeez. It's still there. I just wanted you to know that they might replace them with solar-powered ones. It's gonna happen. They replaced all of the ones on South Oates with solar-powered models, but they all went out for some reason. Once they figure out why and fix the problem, it's gonna happen."

August nodded and sat back once more, saying, "Don't worry, Bobbo. I'm gonna make some calls. They won't be replacin' those two down on West Main Street. I'll pay a significant amount of Credit to make sure."

-

August opened the door to their old bedroom. Everything looked the same as that day, except the bed had been made. He sat down and remembered the last time he had made love to his wife… to anyone for that matter. It had been right here in this bed, 30 years ago.

Over the years, there had been plenty of opportunities to be with other women, especially as a wealthy bachelor who traveled the world regularly. But he never had the need to be with anyone else because he felt Sam's presence at least once a day when he cooked. And that was better than sex with a stranger.

Woodrow stood in the corner, wearing a navy blue dress with white dots all over it. The baseball cap that said, "Kiss the Cook" was now a little crooked, but the necklace holding Samantha's engagement and wedding rings still looked the same.

August unpacked his bag onto the bed and got to work. 30 years was a long time for any robot to be idle, much less one made of wood. When they had built him, they had known he wouldn't last for very long. He was just wood and string.

But the string was synthetic and strong as steel. It was fine. No maintenance required. The wood, on the other hand, was in need of some love. And that was something August had plenty to give.

A few hours of deliberate and gentle care later, August felt satisfied that Woodrow was up to the challenge. He stepped back and put his hand on his hips while looking the old, wooden robot over from top to bottom.

"Woodrow. Power on," August instructed.

The automaton made of wood stirred to life. His eyes lit up, glowing for just a moment. And then they went out. August's heart fell to the floor. It was supposed to work… it should work. He didn't have a backup plan, this was it.

Frantically he looked at his timepiece and saw the hour was growing late. He rushed to Woodrow and threw open the panel in his chest, revealing the machinery within. The motor was fine. It was titanium and would last forever, basically. The circuit boards, on the other hand, were toast. They had rotted through for some reason.

He looked and tried to figure out why. Then he noticed something missing. Dust. There was no dust on the automaton at all. Not a single speck. Which meant that Holly had eventually been able to clean him.

Looking closer at the circuit boards, he took them out. They fell apart in his hands. No wonder he couldn't power on. August thought carefully. He needed to replace the ruined chips and put in new ones. And he needed to do it quickly.

August rushed back to the workshop where he tore and rummaged through everything inside. He found six of the same circuit boards, the ones he needed, only they were rotted through, as well.

"Where can I find more of these damn boards!" August yelled.

They weren't memory or programmed functions boards. They were power circuits that he designed, so it's not like he could walk down and buy some from the local tech store. August had developed this type of chip when he stole power as a broke twenty-something to power his cellphone. Then he began using them for anything he wanted to be fueled by the Tesla generator outside of town.

"My cellphone!" he shouted in triumph.

August yanked it out of his back pocket and looked at the little cellphone. As he did so, August realized that it was too small. The chip wouldn't fit.

"What else did I use them for in the house?" he asked himself quietly, thinking hard.

"LifeLanterns!" he said.

He had manufactured tons of those chips for his LifeLanterns. He quickly remembered that all of them had been at the shop. He had abandoned the shop, hadn't he? They had all been stolen 30 years ago. But hadn't he bought two LifeLanterns in Thailand? They still worked. He used them all of the time in his bungalow. He just needed to go and...

His bungalow was in Malaysia... on the other side of the world, right? August had forgotten where he was for a minute.

"Fuck! I can't believe this!" he screamed, pounding on the workbench. "I came all the way around the world just to fail? Why, God? Why are you doin' this to me?"

That was when August remembered there were still two working lanterns in this town. He had forgotten what he had asked Bobby to do with them at first, but now he knew exactly where they were.

On West Main Street.

CHAPTER 28
BETWEEN THE LANTERNS

There wasn't enough time to get down to West Main Street, take the boards out of the lanterns, come back here, and then install them. He knew that without question.

August tried to pick the large, wooden automaton up to take Woodrow with him to West Main Street, but there was no way he could carry him all that way. August's mind was all mixed up, and he couldn't think straight. It was incredibly frustrating for him, to say the least.

In his workshop, August once again tore through everything with reckless abandon, not caring what he broke or damaged. He needed to find something... anything... to help him move that robot.

August's eyes went to the back corner of his small workshop. Leaned against the wall, old but hopefully still working, was his old maglev sled. He had used it years ago to move around heavy equipment or junk that he found lying around or in dumpsters.

He pulled it out from behind some boxes full of now use-less tech, and it tipped over, falling towards the floor… and August's feet. If it didn't power on, it was all over. That sled weighed more than he did, and it would crush his feet and legs, leaving August incapable of going anywhere.

The maglev sled hummed to life and floated a foot off of the ground. August breathed a heavy sigh of relief. He gently guided it into the bedroom and, as carefully as possible, moved Woodrow's prone form onto the sled. Once positioned well enough, August didn't waste any time.

Out the front door, August moved the hovering sled as fast as he could over to his AutoCar. He hated driving one, and preferred to use bicycles, but his knees weren't up to the challenge much anymore. August shoved, pushed, pulled, and struggled to get the wooden robot into the back seat, and eventually succeeded.

The magnetic levitating sled went into the trunk, and August peeled off faster than he should on this street. He should really slow down. There were children in this neighborhood.

Racing through traffic, he swerved to dodge in between slow-moving AutoCars whose owners weren't paying any attention to the road. They were too caught up in a good book, a movie, or news vids.

August wanted to run every red light but thought better of it. If he were to be pulled over right now, it would be tragic... absolutely tragic.

As he turned onto West Main Street, his heart raced faster than it should for a man of his age. He drove down to the very end of the downtown strip, all the way down past the bars and restaurants. All the way down past the clinic, the Baptist church, and the new office buildings.

And that's when he saw them. The two lanterns hung motionless in the air, levitating like all the other ones in New Dothan. There was nothing outwardly unique about them. They gave off the same light, fueled by the Tesla generator outside of town, providing pure, clean, wireless energy.

No poles were holding them in place. The magnetic levitation plates on the bottom kept them at the perfect ten feet above the automated sidewalks. They were just normal, everyday lanterns. And between them is where he and Samantha had met for the very first time.

August's heart skipped a beat as he saw them and then looked at the spot on the road where he had first met, and then later kissed, the most perfect human ever put on this wretched planet.

There were no parking spaces available, of course, but he didn't care. August pulled as close to the spot as he could and threw the car in park. He left it running and left his door open as he ran back to the trunk to remove the maglev sled.

He began extracting Woodrow from the back seat of his AutoCar. It was slow-going, and a few people passed by. No one offered the old man any help, of course. Typical.

August eventually got Woodrow out and pushed the sled into the middle of the street, directly in between the lanterns... The lanterns that hovered 10 feet above him.

"How am I going to get them down?" August whispered.

They were far out of his reach. He grabbed at his gray hair and pulled, trying to pry any ideas out of that once razor-sharp mind. His breathing slowed and his pupils dilated as a memory crept back into his mind. He looked up and knew that, although they looked the same as the other street lanterns in New Dothan, they weren't the same. He had modified these two unique lanterns.

Hoping beyond all hope that they still functioned correctly, he called out to the lanterns. Would they still recognize his voice commands after all these years?

"Lanterns, lower to four feet off the ground, and dim lights to 50%, please and thank you."

For a twisted and torturous second, the lanterns didn't move. They stayed right where they were, 10 feet above the ground.

But then they made a whirring noise, and their light dimmed to half of what it was. And thankfully, they floated down to four feet off the ground, exactly as August had told them to do.

Again, August wasted no time, as that was a resource he was quickly running out of. Opening both up, and disconnecting the power boards, the lanterns went out but remained floating. The magnetic levitation didn't run off Tesla power, but the ability to alter the strength or weakness of the levitation was now gone, along with the lights.

Finally, he had the boards he would need to get Woodrow back up and running. They were in fantastic shape, as they had not been subjected to whatever it was that damaged the rest of the boards.

He opened the panel in the newly cleaned and maintained wooden robot's chest. The two slots were still empty from where he had removed the damaged boards back at the house.

With expert care, scared to break the last remaining boards like this in North America, he placed them into their respective ports inside of Woodrow. August then closed the chest panel and stepped back. He crossed his fingers for luck and said, "Woodrow. My old friend. Power on."

A car horn suddenly blared, scaring the bejesus out of August. Flashbacks of being hit by an AutoCar 30 years ago flickered through his mind. The resulting injuries twinged in his arm and ribcage as he braced himself for the impact.

But the impact never came. He spun around to see a teenager leaning out of the window of a very new and expensive AutoCar.

"Get out of the road, you crazy old bastard! I'm late!" the young hooligan yelled at the top of his lungs.

August laughed nervously, nodded his head, and replied, "Sorry about that, youngin'. Please just go around me."

Gesturing to the side, August heard a sound like a load of freshly chopped wood being dropped by the fireplace.

"GO AROUND," Woodrow added, gesturing to the side.

August whirled around as fast as his old bones would permit. There, standing upright and looking like no time had passed at all, was the wooden automaton he and his beautiful wife had built a lifetime ago.

Fresh tears fell from August's eyes as he ignored the loud teenager asking ignorant questions about what the hell that mahogany thing was. August had only one thing on his mind, and no one would distract him from this long-awaited reunion.

Reaching into his pocket, August pulled out the SameSoul. The little box that had changed the world, that had changed his life, and most importantly... that held the essence and consciousness of his long-dead love. He looked at the little box and the port on Woodrow where it belonged. And August hesitated.

This was wrong. There was a reason he had never done it. Samantha hated the idea of being inside a machine, even Woodrow. She wouldn't want him to do this even now, after years of being away from him and being in... Heaven?

All of a sudden August felt something familiar inside of him. It was the same humming, electrical feeling in his chest as when he cooked… the radiance that he knew to be Samantha communicating with him from… somewhere.

And he knew right then, that it was ok. The feeling… or Samantha… was telling August that it was ok to put the SameSoul into Woodrow. And so he did. August slid it into place until it clicked.

The light in Woodrow's eyes went out for a split second and then came back on as a slightly different color.

"Hey, sweets," a familiar, long-gone voice said to August. "You got old."

It was her voice. It was Samantha's voice. A sound he had not heard in what seemed like forever. August fell to his knees and buried his face in his hands as he wept.

"Hey, now, sweets," the voice said. "Get up. It's ok. Don't worry. I'm here, I've got you."

Smooth, wooden hands reached out and gently pulled August to his feet. They were surprisingly strong but incredibly delicate. He raised his eyes and looked into the lights emanating from the wooden automatons' sockets, and knew that his wife was inside… looking out at him. That realization brought a happy smile to his face. One so big it almost hurt.

August embraced the wooden vessel, squeezing as hard as he could, and said, "I've missed you so much, Sam. I've hurt so much… and felt your loss for so long. I never even got to say goodbye..." he admitted, which made his voice grow tight with sadness. "It's haunted me for 30 years, babe."

The wooden hands rubbed on his back, exactly the way Samantha had done when she was alive. It felt different, but still warmed August's heart beyond what he thought possible anymore.

"I'm so sorry, sweets," she cooed. "I didn't want to hurt you. I never wanted that. I was scared that maybe I was wrong about God... and Heaven. I wanted our last hours together to be happy ones. I never could have predicted that you'd get hit by a damn car, just like John."

August pulled back and feigned surprise, tears still falling down his cheeks, and said, "You doubted the Divine? Ooooh, I'm tellin', girl."

Samantha laughed. It was her exact same laugh, a sound August had missed as much as a fish misses water on dry land. And hearing it made everything instantly better.

And then August collapsed onto the road.

There was no pain, only the loss of muscle control. He could still see, he could still talk, but August couldn't move.

"Ouch," he moaned.

"Sweets!" Samantha's voice said from within the wooden automaton. "What in Heaven's name is happening?"

August looked at his beautiful wife. Her long, black hair fell to her shoulders, and that cute spread of freckles on her cheeks stood out in the Alabama dusk light.

But that wasn't right. It was Woodrow looking down at him. He was so confused.

"I think it's my time, babe," August said, as quiet as a mouse. "My Countdown ends today."

Those gentle, wooden hands caressed August's face and chest, and her voice whispered, "Oh sweets. Why did you wait so long?"

His breathing grew uneven, and August saw the navy blue dress with white dots all over it that clung sexily to her beautiful figure underneath. She hadn't aged a single day since her death. How was that possible?

But wait... that wasn't right...

"I wanted to respect your wishes, Sam," August tried to explain quickly, as he knew time was growing shorter with every beat of his failing heart. "I know you gave me a choice and all, but I wasn't gonna do anythin' you didn't really want."

"You old dummy," Samantha said, her voice somehow sounding full of sadness. "It's alright, though. I was always with you, sweets. In the SameSoul."

August's unfocused eyes regained a momentary shine as he said, "So that was you, every time I cooked... and just now? That feeling... it was you the whole time?"

The wooden automaton did its best approximation of a shrug, and Samantha's beautiful voice said, "It's hard to explain, sweets. I was aware of you... your presence... and when you cooked I felt happy. Sometimes I felt this other presence, too. It was trying to pull me somewhere. Somewhere I couldn't go just yet, not without you. I don't know. But just now when you were thinking of not putting the SameSoul into old Woodrow, I knew that you had to. I... I tried to yell your name, I think. Like I said. It's real hard to explain."

August felt a peaceful and warm sensation wash over him, but it was getting hard to see... and to breathe. August began gasping for air. He felt everything going numb, starting down at his toes. August realized that he was dying.

"Sam," he said quietly but desperately, "does that mean that there is a Heaven? Is there something after this? Will I get to see you again, babe?"

The gentle, wooden hands wiped tears from August's face, and her gentle voice said, "I'm sorry, sweets. I don't know."

August Lurie closed his eyes. But before his final breath left his lungs, Samantha Lurie leaned close and said, "But we're going to find out together."

Opening one last time, August's eyes beheld their final sight ever. His wife was holding a little black box in her hand.

"I love you more than there are stars in the universe, August," Samantha said.

August's voice caught in his throat, but he croaked through it, and said, "I love you more than there are grains of sand on every beach on every planet in this and all other universes."

As the last rattling breath finally escaped from her husband's lungs, Samantha Lurie, or Woodrow... or maybe both of them... crushed the little black box to dust.

The Tesla generator outside of town suddenly shut down and all of the lights in New Dothan went out instantaneously. Seconds later the town's new solar array, one the size of a football field, powered on for the first time. And all of the lights in New Dothan came back on, except for two.

THE END

www.ingramcontent.com/pod-product-compliance
Lightning Source LLC
Chambersburg PA
CBHW020242180626
46810CB00006B/2317